Prologue-

"All the world's a stage and all the men and women merely players. They have their exits and their entrances. And one man plays many parts." AS YOU LIKE IT – William Shakespeare

Our role changes as time goes on. We are Cast into our role and, as our roles change we are Cast into new roles.

The director Casting the players may be seen as circumstance, government, or God. Each player performs as placed on the stage of life. Each player performs as trained or taught. The stage is set and….

The play goes on!

Characters:

The Black Robes (judges)

The Chosen One (President)

The Elite (Congress)

The Movement (underground workers)

The Cast (producers, those who build, service, and keep economy going, and those banned from society)

Transport Cast

Housing Cast

Food Cast

Media Cast

Communications Cast

Construction Cast

Medical Cast

Education Cast

Out Cast (the stage outside society)

Etc.

The Elect (banned groups of believers)

The forbidden (all communication, written and spoken, that contradicts the Elite or Chosen One)

Fli - a member of the Elite Cast who is in The Movement.

Each society Cast is defined and controlled by the Elite. Who gains admittance, who gets which job, who is terminated from the Cast, who leads or drives the Cast… all is determined by the Elite.

The Elite define require payments from those who have been endowed with a job by the elite. These payments are set by production standards with an amount allocated to the worker for needs. This is very similar to farming on a share crop basis. The owner receives all the income and pays the sharecropper in food and housing

plus some benefits. This keeps
the sharecropper tied to the plow
as there is never enough to get
ahead or out of the situation.

All requests for food, clothing,
housing, etc. are required to go
to the Elite for approval.

All health care must be received
from Elite chosen Cast,
irrespective of the ability of the
Cast member.

Any location change must be
approved by the Elite. Location
changes required by the Elite must
be done or the Elite cuts off all
ability to work and all
subsistence.

All society Casts are trained to
turn to the Elite for everything.
The Elite run a controlled economy
where everyone is "taken care of".

All are required to submit to the decisions of the Elite.

The Movement focuses on the Constitution of the United States as adopted in 1791 and the written Word of God. Documents are memorized by many, stored in secret locations, and forbidden by the Elite.

The Elect work within the Movement, keeping identities secret.

The Elite is composed of members of secret societies who have formed a common goal and strengths. Separation of Church and State has formally become Separation of church from state. The right to keep and bear arms has been reduced from keeping the military in line, to be possessed only by the military in order to keep the Cast in line. Freedom of speech has been changed so only speech in favor of the Elite is guaranteed. Any speech that brings a negative view of the Elite is forbidden

THE STAGE

Entree-

"I should introduce myself. I am seen as one of the Elite Cast. I am also a Fli a member of the Movement who gathers and passes information within the Movement. There are few of us among the Elite. If we are found out we are sent to the Out Cast."

"The ability to get food or clothing or shelter in the society is withdrawn. The society has progressed to the point that the death penalty no longer exists. Those who do not conform to the system are simply allowed to starve or to "escape" beyond the fence to be attacked by wild animals."

"I am able to move freely through society as I can assume the uniform of any Cast and mix. As I do this I also take on many names. Each Cast has been assigned names that are unique to that Cast. In this way the Elite keep track of the Casts and keep control. I might define a Fli so you can understand the danger. A Fli is a person who works to help individuals in any Cast who find the need to find freedom and the ability to be on their own. Not many have the will to give up everything that is provided but there are those who seek to get out of the Cast they have been assigned to and trained in from birth. Each Fli works alone but has the ability to pass an individual to another Fli in an "underground" movement, until the person is in the hands of the elect."

"I have been sent on spy missions to find the Elect. This is how I became a Fli. I learned about the joy they have in the freedom to live with choices and grow in many abilities. Expressions on their faces and the openness of their body language were like a lighted sign saying "We have happiness". I was one of the few spies to make contact with the Elect."

"When the fences were erected (to keep the wild animals out), there were those who had been able to remain free, outside the fences. These were the Elect. They set up a system of helping those Out Cast to start a free life and to teach them the skills to be an asset to

their society. They were not only
to survive but to produce for
others. In this way those who had
crop failures or illness and
couldn't survive alone had help
until they would have better crops
or recover from their illness."

It was an old custom, started by
Christians over a thousand years
ago. They took time to talk to
God six times a day. Each hour
was set aside for a particular
focus. Night prayer was focused
on thanking God for the previous
day's help and asking him to help
and protect those under the Elite.
Early morning prayer was set aside
to thank God for their families
and the Elect and to ask for
protection for them. Prayer at
dawn was focused on thanking God
for another day and another
opportunity to serve him and
others. Mid day prayer was set

aside to ask for the strength to continue as he guides. Afternoon prayer was set aside to ask for the grace to be bestowed on all the Elect. Evening prayer was set aside to ask for a secure and restful night.

Although the times were passed down and taught, the form of prayer differed. At times, when work was slow, an hour might be spent. At other times a short sentence or two was always heard. It wasn't the volume but the content that was taught.

I had gone into the wilderness to search for the Elect and found myself camping close to a stream. In the morning breakfast was set out. There was no one there but the smells and flavors of the food were like nothing I had experienced before. Food in this desert place was also nothing I expected to experience. I decided that I had made "contact" and that I did not need to search further. I continued to camp until one of the Elect made his presence known by walking into camp one morning. He was waiting for me when I woke up.

That meeting was different. He had the food ready as the days before. He was sitting at the side of the clearing calmly waiting without making a sound. Beside him, lying on the ground, was a large dog. They simply waited while I ate and continued waiting until I spoke to the man. I hadn't learned to talk to dogs so ignored his friend. The man introduced himself as Ariean. He and a friend had brought the food. Ariean wanted to know what I was looking for and where I was going.

I told him I was looking for the
Elect. Then, I would return to
society and report. Ariean asked
me if I would report factual
information or filtered
information. I couldn't say.
Ariean guided me to the Elect.

The next weeks were a patchwork
of experiences. Each night Ariean
and his friend Alehandra took me
to a different location. At each
stop we were met by a group of the
Elect. They provided hospitality,
food and comfort (which were
needed after a long night's ride).
I learned later that the dog went
ahead and notified the group that
we would be there the next
morning. They would ask about
particular individuals in the
Society. They showed deep concern
about the welfare of all, but
seemed to have certain interest in
specific individuals. I surmised

that these were those they had
worked with or known in their own
Cast.

As to my report, I will say that
it was filtered. I did not report
the enjoyment I had in their
presence. I did not report the
hospitality I received or their
interest about those in society.
I simply reported that I traveled
many days and found the Elect to
be scattered and few. Although
this may not be accurate, it was
true to my experience.

The following is a record of
some of my observations as I moved
in and out of the Casts in
society. Much of the
understanding of the thought
processes of those observed was
gained much later. They are
interwoven so you can understand
more fully how they thought and

reacted to the society and the
Elite Cast.

Chapter 1

Andi slid out of bed. It was
Sunday morning, the first day of
the week. "I need to get ready
for work. Things used to be
different from the under-stories I
overheard occasionally told by the
Workers Cast. Back then Sunday
was considered sacred and set
aside for those who wished to
honor God. There were even "blue
laws" forbidding certain
activities and certain sales."

That was a long time ago. The
Elite pushed for reforms to
increase productivity. All
businesses are now open every day.
Each employee works a four day
week on a rotating schedule. This
allows each business to hire more
employees. The Manufacturing Cast
is tasked to keep the machinery
running 20 hours a day. Four

hours each day are set aside for maintenance. Two shifts of ten hours keep the production lines going. The Elite optimized the system for full output. They still haven't figured out how to handle unexpected machinery failures. Andi gets ready for work and sits down for a quick breakfast. "Meals are easy to fix. There are six options for each meal which comes prepackaged from the Food Cast." They are designed to heat and eat. "If I am in a hurry and don't mind cold meals they are consumable cold". This is handy when in a hurry. The Elite designed the meals to have the proper nutrition and calories for each Cast scientifically designed to provide the necessities. Casts that require more manual labor have meals with more calories. The meals are optimized for a healthy society. They haven't figured out why sickness continues to affect the Casts.

"I will clean the dishes and place them into the return packet before I leave for work." Each week the meals for the week come in a packet. That packet with the recycled dishes is returned each week when the Casts go to the Food Cast distribution center for the weekly packet.

Every work day is the same. Andi walks the mile to the Transport Cast pick up station where she catches the transporter to work. The pick-up stations are placed so most of the workers need to walk a good distance to and from the station, requiring the needed exercise. Andi gets four hours of walking in going to and from work each work cycle. This regimen of walking and breathing fresh air helps workers live a healthier life.

As the transporter arrives Andi climbs on board. "There are two other passengers", she notices. "It will be thirty minutes before the car is completely filled with Casts going to work." Andi can tell by their uniform the type of work they did. In order to increase production and reduce costs the Elite requires each cast to wear the same style clothes. This is intended to reduce the feeling of individuality and increased the feeling of belonging to a productive Cast. The feeling of achievement is to be as a member of a group rather than as an individual. The idea is, this will prompt the Cast members to encourage each other to be productive.

Andi arrives at work, focused on getting through the next four days. The Communications Cast workers around her are unsmiling. "The atmosphere feels like the model train I saw in a museum once. The passengers were lifeless and the train went around and around and really went nowhere." The "news" is written by the Elite and distributed by them. The task of the Communications Cast is to distribute the information to the Casts. Survival depends on accurately transmitting the messages of the Elite to the Casts. Any information that could be misinterpreted will be relegated to interviews. This allows the Elite to personally address the Casts and any misunderstanding is then not the fault of the Communication Cast.

Andi goes to her station and reviews the messages from the Elite. "There are the standard messages on getting production up. There are the standard notices on working for the good of Society. There are the standard messages about how The Chosen One and the Elite were taking care of the Society, bringing all together in uniformity. There is something different in the stack." The Chosen One is asking everyone to build the neighborhood. "The Elite have been great benefactors. Employment is up. Each worker works but 4 days a week. This leaves three days for the Casts to work together to build the neighborhood. We expect each individual to find an area where that individual can help

strengthen the neighborhoods.
Reports of activity and successes
will be sent to the office of the
Elite each month describing the
activity each individual
undertakes along with three
signatures of neighbors verifying
the activity. We expect each
individual to contribute ten hours
a week building the neighborhood."

Andi sees the challenge to the
Communications Cast. The message
not only needs to be given to all
the Casts but it has to be given
in a way that is workable and
encouraging. "Our job is to
implement the desires of The
Chosen One and the Elite."

With rotating shifts, she has
the same days off as each
individual in her neighborhood
about twice a year. That means
that a neighborhood can be

introduced to each other in six months. Andi thinks, "How are they expected to work together? Maybe the Communications Cast can set up a neighborhood bulletin board or a weekly notice of what is going on in the neighborhood. But this opens the risk of being misunderstood by the Elite and having neighbors becoming Out Cast."

As always, the Elite formulates ideas without considering the challenges for implementing those ideas. The workers in a neighborhood quickly realize that they are being tasked to do the impossible. At least, they are being told to do the improbable. The penalty for failure was always present. The food allotment is reduced. The ability to take the train is withdrawn. The Society

exists to follow the directions of
the Elite.

Andi knows the challenges both
the Communications Cast and the
workers face. She can not express
these ideas or address them to the
Elite. That would be
unforgivable.

Chapter 2

   Andrew and Mary had lived a good
life. Their parents had kept the
Sabbath their entire lives. When
The Chosen One took over, the
right to openly believe was taken
away. It started with public
prayer. First those who worked
for the government in any way were
banned from any public prayer
while on the job. When the ban
was complete, they were allowed to
go to a church and express their
beliefs in the church building.
This was called "freedom of
worship". They were banned from
any display of belief in God
outside the church buildings.
After the ban on government
employees, came the ban on any
public expression of religious
beliefs. Everyone was confined to
expression within the churches
only. This was to protect the

rights of the non-believers from being exposed to God. Then non-believers started going into the churches and their "rights" were violated there also. The Elite then closed the churches and banned any conversation or display of belief in God.

Andrew and Mary chose to believe. They were found out and sent to the Out Cast. They went with the Elect. They had little information of what happened to the society. Occasionally, a Fli would visit and update them. This was always risky as the Fli could be discovered and made an Out Cast.

Life with the Elect is freeing. As long as The Chosen One and the Elite are busy trying to keep control of the society they have neither the resources nor desire

to pursue the Elect. Producing
their own food and working
together out of mutual necessity
and trust builds a strong
community. Choosing to depend on
each other, or learning who not to
depend on, gives meaning to their
everyday lives.

Andrew and Mary live as their
great grandparents had many years
ago. They till and plant using
mules and horses. They walked or
ride the mules or horses to go
places. They gather with the
community on Sunday to praise God
and to renew their covenant with
Him. They help each other through
disasters, troubles and crop
failures.   It is a hard but
fulfilling life.

They are free of the control of
The Chosen One and the Elite.
They have no fear of being Out

Cast without the skills to survive. They are Out Cast with the skills to survive. These they have learned from other Out Casts when they arrived outside the fence.

Andrew and Mary left children behind. They hadn't known the former life when the final change occurred. They wanted the safety of the society. They complied and cooperated. Andrew and Mary lost touch and hadn't heard how they were doing for many years. The family had been divided.

Home is a small cabin, constructed of logs and straw. Each log is split lengthwise twice (height and width) then the sides are squared off to form a square board. One wall is stacked and locked together to form the outer wall and another wall is stacked

and locked to form an inner wall.
The twelve inches between the
walls are then filled with straw.
The straw is compressed to form
insulation. The outside is then
covered with boards cut to make
siding. This keeps rain from
getting between the logs and to
the straw. The straw insulates so
the wind doesn't get through.
Glass for windows comes at a
premium. It has to be acquired
from the society. Since this is
not legal, accommodations have to
be made. Usually, a piece of
glass that is broken is scheduled
for discard. This is then
"disposed of" where the elect
carries it off and cuts off the
good parts for use.

   The soil is good and the water
from the stream is plentiful.
With that in mind, they grow two
crops. One is for their use and

the other is for barter and
helping others who need help.
Those who need help also come over
to help with the planting or
harvest. There were a few who
help anytime they are needed.
This is the way they had been
taught.

Meat is plentiful. The Elite
took control of all health care
and banned meat from the diet.
This was to reduce the number of
heart and circulatory problems.
Smoking was banned also. Anyone
caught with smoking tobacco or
meat is cut off from all health
care. When this happens the only
way to survive is to find a way to
the Elect. They have skilled
physicians who know the skills to
treat diseases that are unknown to
the Medical Cast. The Medical
Cast was trained to focus on
prevention and had become

preventionists. When an illness
does occur their skills are
limited.

   Andrew and Mary have an
abundance of animal life to add to
their garden produce for a well
rounded diet. The incidence of
health illnesses formerly caused
by the fats in meat does not
affect the Elect. They have
adopted a lifestyle that is labor
intensive. With all the exercise
the meat does not have the effect
it does in a sedentary society.

Chapter 3

Dan is trying to sleep. The second shift is just starting in his rotation. It will take a few days for him to adjust to the change. It seems that life is a constant adjustment. If the Elite planned for the workers to work on a shift permanently, they would adjust and do better. It is their fairness doctrine that says no worker should have a better time schedule than any other worker. Everyone works rotating shifts and everyone lives a life of trying to get their body adjusted to the new shift, just in time to be rotated to a new shift. Everyone is uniformly miserable.

Sleep comes slowly. Although Dan's internal clock is saying that it is time to get up, he needs to get his sleep. By the

time he finally drifts off to
sleep he gets only a few short
hours of sleep before having to
get up to go work again.
Accidents at work are common.
When they occur they became short-
handed and work slows down. It is
better to work slowly and be
careful so accidents can be
avoided. This takes some doing,
working slowly while seeming to
work fast. Intentional slow downs
could mean disciplinary actions,
loss of benefits, and being
stigmatized as a loafer.
Construction doesn't keep up to
the goals set by the Elite. The
Construction Cast are skilled at
survival. The equipment doesn't
get the maintenance needed, only
the maintenance authorized. The
waiting list is long for
buildings, transporters, and
services like electricity, water,

sewer, and heat. As a
disciplinary action, these are
provided last to the Construction
Cast. This is the Elite's way of
saying they aren't doing their
job.

Getting up, Dan fixes the
provided meal. It isn't the
standard Construction meal. The
Elite determined that slow workers
needed less nutrition. The meals
are lower on calories and
nutrients than for those who
perform manual labor each day.
This is how Dan goes to work each
day, working to keep enough energy
to get home and sleep after each
shift. Taking the transporter to
work Dan notices the little things
on the transporter that need
maintenance. He knows the
maintenance will not get done.
There are few maintenance workers
and they can not keep up with the

needed repairs. One day this
transporter will simply stop
working and those who depended on
it to get to work will hope that a
replacement will be available. As
it is, the same transporter serves
two to three routes, carrying
workers to and from work. The
shifts are adjusted accordingly so
they are picked up and dropped off
as the transporter is available.

  Dan looks at the other
passengers. Their uniforms tell
him which Cast they are assigned
to. He notices the weariness on
their faces and the way they
embark and disembark. The lack of
hope permeates all the Casts.
That, they have in common.

  Dan disembarks at his station to
walk the mile to his work. Along
the way he notices the lack of
color. Gardens are for produce

only but they are restricted to
the Elite and Olders. Having a
garden violates the ability of the
Elite to control the food intake
of the Casts. The Olders had
survived to the point they can no
longer work. They are allowed to
have gardens so they can produce
much of their own food and not be
a drain on the produce of the Farm
Cast. The Farm Cast is controlled
to carefully produce what is only
necessary. It was determined that
too many Farm Cast would take away
from the more important Casts.
Besides that, the Farm Cast works
on rotating shifts and there were
times the work isn't timely as the
time to harvest happens between
shifts or when the workers on
shift don't have the skills to do
the job. Food to the kitchens is
lean more often than not. The
Olders are required to garden in

order to survive and to help take the load off the Farm Cast. The few gardens along his walk have no flowers. The colors and plants that help brighten the day had been deemed extraneous and unnecessary. The water to grow them is too precious to waste.

   Dan arrives at work to find his machine had broken the previous shift. It is scheduled for maintenance in thirty days. Dan goes to find someone who works a machine like his. If he could "help" and look busy they might not cut his rations again. He needs to "work" during his shift so the Elite will reward him. These are the really tough days. It is hard enough to keep his own machine working. To make someone else appear to need his help might put them on the list and both might be hurt. They both know the risk and are willing to help each other seem to "work". They are thankful that the Elite know little about the machines or what it really takes to operate them. All they are concerned about is the end result. When it suffers all the workers suffer together. When a machine brakes down every shift is affected.

Each machine is used twenty hours a day and the Maintenance Cast maintains the equipment the other four hours each day. This is considered the optimum usage. The machine does not sit idle and is able to give maximum production. There is a shortage of the Maintenance Cast which causes the maintenance on the machines to be overlooked.

Dan is able to keep busy during his shift. He wants to warn the person that replaces him on the following shift. The Elite scheduled shifts to prevent "idle talk" between shifts. Dan doesn't know his replacement. One day he thought he saw her coming to work. At least he thought the person he saw approaching his machine is his counterpart on the following shift. She could have been filling in for one who had been sent to The Farm. Dan is expected to keep to his business and not be concerned about the others. The only information he gets is what the Elite provided. Mostly, this is about how well they were doing in running the society. Aside from that there are the forbidden bits and pieces overheard about those called the Elect.

Dan is able to figure out that the Elect are not a Cast. They are spoken of as anti-society. These

are the ones that set themselves
up to go against the will of the
Elite. Dan had heard that they
have no privileges, no food
allowance, no housing provided, no
jobs and no benefits. Dan
wondered why anyone would end up
so lost and how they could
survive.

Chapter 4

Andi goes over the reports at the beginning of each day. The news is focused on how the society functions better than the past system. There is no crime reported. No one is injured. The sick are rare. The elderly are taken care of.

Andi went to work. The headlines read "The Elite have authorized vacations for those who have made this society the most productive in history". The story reads that all of the parts of society are producing beyond expectations. Food supplies are in abundance. Factories continue to produce at full capacity. Supplies are available for all occupations. Students are learning more than they had in the past. The productivity is so well

coordinated that workers are to be
given a well earned vacation.
Neighborhood get-togethers are
being organized so the vacation
can be enjoyed by celebrating
together. Those living in a
neighborhood will be able to get
to know each other. With
neighbors getting to know each
other, the feeling of safety and
security is strengthened. Andi
reads the report. It is necessary
to publish it accurately, so the
Elite will be satisfied. On the
way to work Andi observed
machinery standing idle,
construction ground to a halt,
workers performing busy work so as
to look productive. Everywhere
she looks the system is falling
apart. It is a challenge to
muster the strength to report the
"party line". It appears the
Elite are instituting a "vacation"

to give time to fix the problems
so everyone can go back to work.
Andi sits down to write the story
the headlines announced. Some
occupations are stressful. Andi
had been assigned to one of those.
It will be a long day.

Chapter 5

Ariean spends a lot of time by the
stream. It is peaceful there.
The fields around the stream are
filled with wild flowers of all
sorts. The colors brighten the
days. When a breeze flows over
the flowers, he sees colors in
motion, like life flowing across
the fields. There are times he
would sit still and enjoy the
natural beauty. At these times,
he would often see a deer, or wild
turkeys, or a pronghorn. Back in
the fields he would see pheasants
or quail.

Here, at the stream, Ariean spends
hours fishing. He would catch
enough for his family and also
enough to share with others who
didn't have the skill to catch
their own. Today, Ariean already

has a dozen pan sized fish in the
bucket. It isn't noon yet. He
will catch a few more, clean one
and cook it over a small fire for
lunch, then enjoy the peaceful
colors before heading back to
their home.

It was written that there is a
time for everything under the sun.
Ariean's time for fishing is
Tuesdays and Fridays. On these
days he caught what could be used
in three days. Sometimes there is
more than needed and these are
cooked and dried for when they
will be needed, like the overlook
times.

   Late in the afternoon Ariean
gathers his pole and bucket and
heads back home. He stops by a
couple of the neighbors along the
way and gives them fish. When he

gets home, he proceeds to clean and prepare the fish. They are cooked that night and those that aren't set aside for the meal are smoked or dried to preserve them for the next two days. Tomorrow will be another task and another day. Ariean's sleep that night is relaxing and refreshing.

The next day Ariean proceeds to fix fence around the fields. Although they enjoy the wild life and harvest some for their meat, the Elect also need their fields to produce for their food. Wildlife can eat elsewhere. The fences are an invitation to leave this food alone. However, the wildlife find the fare more palatable and easier to get in the fields. This makes the fences necessary. They always seem to need repair.

The first field has two breaks
and he has these fixed by noon.
Alehandra is always ready to help.
She carries the supplies and keeps
him company while he fixes the
fences. They walk the fences
together, sometimes sharing a
light moment. Some of those
moments could be humorous.
Alehandra is a good worker but she
seems to always be hungry. They
will stop to rest and Ariean will
relieve the field of some of the
choicest produce and share with
Alehandra.

There are times Ariean let his
thoughts wander. He would be
thinking of the coming winter or
the food supply or the hunting or
his family while walking along.
This tends to slow him down.
Alehandra gives him a shove,
sending him stumbling a few steps,
and reminding him they had work to

do. Ariean playfully shoves the
Mule back and they are on their
way again. They need to keep
moving if they are to walk all the
fences each week. They have to be
done on Wednesday and Thursday.
Sunday is set aside for building
their relationship with God.
Monday and Saturday are set aside
for work around the house.

Monday usually finds Ariean
fixing, repairing and cleaning.
When these tasks are done he keeps
busy cutting dead wood, hauling it
to the house, and storing it for
cooking and heating. He had been
taught which types of trees were
best for these uses. Other trees
are better for making furniture
and tools. When the chores are
caught up and Mondays allow the
time, Ariean carves toys for the
children or makes games for the
adults. Mondays are always busy.

Saturday finds Ariean busy helping with the cleaning and cooking. The home is prepared for Sunday and the food is prepared for Sunday. It might be dried or left on the fire to simmer. Occasionally, others would come to share Sunday meals with them or they would go to share meals with someone else. Sunday is not a day of work. Saturday is set aside as a preparation day. However, if there were an emergency and someone needed help on either of these days they set aside their routine to go to the aid of those in need.

It was written that we should feed the hungry, cloth the naked, shelter the homeless, visit the imprisoned, and this was their culture. These needs are to be met when found.

The movement aids the Out Cast to a contact with the Elect. This is a difficult and dangerous undertaking. The Casts ware uniforms. A Cast member who is Out Cast surrenders their uniform and wares clothing indicating they are Out cast. Their movements are restricted. The Society does not border the country of the Elect.

The Out Cast needs to be moved secretly to the border of the Society. Then they are given instructions and directions past the fences. These takes them into the unknown. With few provisions, they travel several days through territory that is foreign to them. There are plants and animals they have never heard of or seen. Their instructions include how to stay safe during this journey.

Some of the Elect watch the exit.
This is the area they have
designated for the Out Cast to
travel out of society. There are
areas the Out Cast will travel
where they could be seen
discretely for miles. The Elect
sends a guide to watch. When the
guide observes Out Cast along the
trail they note the movements,
where they stop, what they do, if
they are followed. If the
instructions are not kept, those
entering into the country would
not find the Elect. The Elite are
known to send out spies to find
the Elect. They have to be
cautious.

   When the Out Cast follow the
route and instructions, an Elect
meets them at night and leads them
to a home where they are be cared
for until they can establish a
home. The journey is at night to

prevent observation. It also makes it difficult for the Out Cast to know how they got there. If they are a spy it will be difficult to get back safely and report.

Even on Sunday a messenger comes to a home and asks for assistance to accept Out Casts. The family will sometimes just need to wait until they arrive. There are times that the Out Cast's health is so poor that they need help getting there. The Elite restricts their food so they had been weakened before the journey started. The few prepared meals they are given before they leave are just enough to keep them alive. Those that give the meals risked being found out if their recycled dished are counted.

Ariean and Alexandra often make a trip to the country to assist the Out Cast. Alexandra carries the wood, utensils and food. When they get to the meeting place Ariean build a cooking fire and prepare a simple meal of fish and stew. When the guide arrives with the Out Cast, Ariean feeds them and lets them rest for a couple of days. The guide then returns along the back trail to make sure they aren't followed and to observe the route again.

Those who volunteer to guide are taught skills that had been lost. They are taught to move swiftly and silently either through the trees or on the plains. They learn to use their ears to listen to sounds of nature and to detect movement and sounds from quite a distance. Their sense of smell is trained to be heightened. The scent of a presence puts them on guard. They also work with a partner. A trained dog is always with them. On the trail, the dog is out in front and on guard. There are many spies who pass within inches of the guard and dog without ever knowing they are there.

After the spies pass, the guard checks their back trail. If it is clear, he follows them. When they camp for the night, he makes a side trip and coordinates with the guide. When they wake up in the morning, they find food waiting for them. This hospitality is both unknown and frightening. Where did it come from? Who had been in their camp? Spies rarely make more than one trip into the unknown. The combination of unexpected hospitality and the uncertainty of the unknown are

hard to understand. Nothing in
their world taught them the grace
of hospitality. Why would the
"enemy" be nice to a stranger?
That, without an explanation,
causes consternation.

   Ariean was one of those who
provides the food for the guide to
take to the camp. It is hard for
the Society to understand the
abilities of the Elect. When the
guide starts trailing the spies he
sends his dog to the Elect for
back up. When the dog arrives
food is loaded quickly and the dog
is followed. They might travel
miles before they meet the guide.
Then they prepare the meal far
away from the spy camp. The guide
then goes with his dog to the camp
and waits until all were asleep
before delivering the meal. If
they have a night watch the dog
distracts the watch while the

guard delivers the food. The
watch does not see the dog; only
hear sounds away from the camp
that keep his attention.

Ariean learned much from the Out
Cast over the years. He knows the
diets and restrictions. He knows
that spies hadn't experienced
"real food". He also knows that
they hadn't experienced anyone who
would help without expecting
something in return. It was
written "feed the hungry". The
Society banned those writings and
the Casts have not been taught
this powerful gift. Ariean is
told by the guards that the spies
returned to the society with a
change in their life. Some could
not readjust and later became Out
Cast.

Chapter 6

Lionia is a good worker. She has remained healthy and never misses work. She does her exercises and kept her strength, and she was fortunate to work in the education Cast. They met their goals. The Elite rewarded them with the necessary food and housing.

Lionia walks a mile to the transport she takes to work. It will take her within a mile of her work. She will then walk to work. The children are taught by Cast. The skills, the language, the proper way to respond to the requests of the Elite are taught by Cast. Lionia is trained to teach the Housing Cast. She is in the lower levels where the specific language and political manners are the emphasis. The Housing Cast learns basic mathematics. Money has long since disappeared so the focus is on populations.

The Housing cast is responsible for coordinating the proper housing for each Cast. This is more difficult than is seems. Each housing district has been designed for diversity. With the diversity in Casts few of the neighbors work in the same Cast. Since the communication is different for each Cast there is great difficulty even getting to know the neighbors. The Elite designed this, they said, to promote diversity. In their initial planning, a major goal was to keep any Cast from getting too strong and causing problems. It is primarily a way of controlling the population.

The housing Cast receives the numbers of needed housing from the Elite. They get the numbers by Cast. It is their job to provide housing (by filling any empty houses or building new ones) by Cast and with diversity. Building several units in one area is a thing of the past. Units are added to existing districts so as to spread out those in a particular cast and promote "diversity". Knowing the number of each Cast in each district, along with the number of new units needed for each Cast, make the calculations fairly simple. Dispersing those in a Cast is the goal.

Lionia is a good teacher. Her students learn the value of working for the Elite. They learn that children of a Cast become workers in that Cast. They learn that it is good for children to live in dormitories while in school so their parent can work. They also learn the education prepares them for working and that the housing they get will be away from their parent.

Lionia has a surprise one Friday evening after school. She takes her usual trip to the Food Cast distribution center. Before entering the distribution center Lionia is asked to go to the Child Cast office. The Child Cast is responsible for the children. They coordinate the lives of children from production to entering the work force as adults. Lionia is told she is chosen to spend time at the farm and produce a child for the society. All arrangements have been made and

Lionia will receive instructions
at the end of the current term.

The farm is self-contained. The
visitors do not walk the miles for
work. They do not live in sparse
quarters. They do not need to go
to the Cast distribution center
for food. They focus on regular
exercise, a good diet, and the
production of children.

Participants are evaluated for
the traits needed to produce
healthy and strong society
members. Both family history and
genetics research limit the
percent of babies with problems.
In the past, genetic engineering
had been used. This proved to be
a failure. Each change seemed to
bring out another weakness. Now
those weak genes are strengthened
by choosing a "father" with
dominant genes to overpower the

weak genes. This is largely successful. However, relapses are always a possibility. Each pairing is chosen as if it was the first.

Lionia arrives at the farm and is checked out. The Farm Cast would determine when she is fertile and plant the donor seed so she can contribute a worker to the society. Implantation is chosen very early as this keeps emotions from interfering. When the father and mother had been brought together an emotional tie often accompanied the fertilization. This led to a disruption of the order of the society. All members need to focus on serving the society. This service to society is weakened by the feeling of exclusivity that grows out of the emotions. Many of the child producers had to be Out Cast when these emotions weakened their service to society. They had disappeared from society. Mary is one of these.

Lionia is introduced to the regimen of the farm. The daily exercises are termed "chores". The daily meals are called "growth enhancements". The daily schedule for sleep and activity is termed "regulation". Lionia will be at the farm from the time she is planted until the child is born. She will then return to her house for a short recovery "leave" before returning to work. As a teacher she will then contribute to society by encouraging her students to be good workers and to stay healthy so they can, in turn, contribute children to society as chosen.

Lionia finds the experience much different than she had been taught. The child growing inside her invades her being. The child is not a mere presence to be carried for society but a living person that is becoming a part of her life, a part that fills a void that has been growing within her for so long.

The child is being loved by Lionia. The love of the mother reaches deep within and touches her child. It is difficult to keep the regimen and not show the change in Lionia's relationship with her child. She knows it is necessary if she is not to be Out Cast.

Life becomes very complex. There were stories she had taught to her students. "Bearing a child is a

privilege to serve the society.
In the past churches imposed the
guilt a woman felt for not being
tied to her child. Women are free
now to bear a child and society
relieves her of the guilt and
responsibility of raising the
child. Women can reach their
great potential, serving society
without the burden of a family
tying her down".

   Lionia is learning the absence
of church and the corresponding
imposition of guilt does nothing
to relieve the feeling she feels
stirring within her. Her training
did not prepare her for the
relationship that was growing
within her. In the periods of
reflection after chores Lionia
wonders if the donor has similar
feelings. The donor does not have
the intimacy of a child within.
The donor has no contact with or

relationship with the woman. He must not experience the caring and love she is experiencing.

Questions fill her hours. Why does something so natural get blamed on a church? When it takes two parties to produce a child what is the natural relationship of the donor? What is life like, to be raised by a mother? What is life like, to be raised by a mother and a donor?

Lionia imagines the life she never had, growing up in a home with a mother who felt towards her the way she is feeling towards her child. Of course that was not possible. Every Adult is required to work in order to be provided for. There is no food or housing, or transportation privileges. Clothing can not be obtained. One who does not work is an Out Cast.

Lionia heard stories about being an Out Cast. People would disappear. Their bodies would not be disposed of so they didn't die. They simply disappeared. The stories hinted that they disappeared beyond the border, without the society network of food, shelter, clothing, secure job, transportation, and the Elite to make the decisions for them. How could they survive in the wilderness? Students learned in school about the wild animals that attack people. The Elite keep wild animals from the society. However, the wild animals exist beyond the border.

Why does the story persist that any Out Cast even exists? Who are they? Why do they leave society? Is it because they can not produce as the Elite required? No, there is a place for those already. The barracks had been set up for those who can not meet production standards. They have shelter and are provided the means to make their own clothing and grow their own food. They help each other and are not be a drain on society. The question persisted, why and who are the Out Cast?

As the months went by and her child grows Lionia grows also. She grows a relationship with her child. Her interest grows in who the donor is and how he feels.

She listens to the conversation around her and keeps picking up fragments of information about the Out Cast. As the farm is situated away from the center of society she can see the land beyond the fence. There are hills covered with trees. There are mountains

in the far distance. And there
are the monthly over flights.

Chapter 7

Andi arrives at work to find
stacks of memos from the Elite.
Wading through these it is
apparent that either the elite are
being kept in the dark or they
feel that the Society needs to be
kept in the dark. Both had
advantages. If they are in the
dark then they are less likely to
hurt the workers who are not as
productive because of equipment
failures. If they are in the know
they are more likely to eliminate
those workers secretly and make it
appear as if the Society were
functioning optimally.

Andi goes to the Bowels to put
her story together. They refer to
it as the Bowels as it is deep
into the depths of the building.
Two levels below the ground level,
it provides quiet and allows for

undisturbed focus on the subject on hand. Andi enjoys the Bowels as few Communications Cast would go there. They feel it is a forbidding environment.

The story comes together quite quickly. It comes easier each time to report anything on a positive note that makes the elite appear good and helpful. Andi looks around and sees the stacks of files that she had seen many times before. She has no desire to read old news. They do not aid her in her reporting. Today is different. She has some time to do research and starts through the stacks. The files are listed by date and by subject. This is like she had heard a library had been. Indexes arrange the files by subject, date, and author. Pick any one of these and research is done efficiently. Entries in the

indexes cease at the time the
Elite gained full control.
However, the events leading up to
the change are interesting.

Andi choses the topic "society"
to begin her studies. In the
early years, the people were
caused distress by government
actions and inactions. The
problems were blamed on the "rich"
and the "employer". Slowly,
"rights" were taken from some and
new "rights" created for others.

The law was redefined in order
to strengthen the poor and weaken
the "rich" (those who had worked
to earn and to save assets).
Taxes were levied on the "rich" to
reduce them to the level of the
poor and make all equal. The
documents described how those in
power kept some poor while blaming
the successful for keeping them

poor. This set up class warfare
and allowed those in power to
continue to undermine the system
and replace it with the Elite.

Slowly, the system that allowed
every individual to have
opportunities to succeed was
transformed into the system that
favored the elite. There was a
treasure of documents forgotten
here. The Elite either forgot the
files were there or had so much
control that they weren't worried
that the files could do harm.
After all, they had been
successful while everyone watched.

Chapter 8

A wellness Cast Fli works in the exercise arena. Going by the name of P.T. the Fli is responsible for the formation, scheduling and operation of the proper exercise program for each visitor. The blood pressure, heart beat, and other body function measurements tell a story. When a visitor is relaxed the measurements tell the story. When the visitor is concerned or worried or deep in thought the measurements tell different stories.

It is important to understand the interaction of the physical being and the inner being to optimize the chores chosen and even the growth enhancements. These can be regulated to optimize the experience. Reduction of stress

and the care of the physical body
is the goal.

P.T. has been working with
Lionia for several months and has
noticed an increase in stress.
This was determined not to be
caused by carrying a child as that
is going smoothly. During her
chores Lionia expresses her
happiness with the chores and the
facility. Something much deeper
is causing the stress. This needs
to be discovered by P.T. in order
to reduce the stress. A consult
needs to be scheduled.

At the consult P.T. might
discuss more personal items with
Lionia. Often a visitor has
second thoughts and the wellness
Cast worker might encourage proper
thinking. The feelings of the
mother for the baby is encouraged
to be understood as a normal

excitement of serving the society. The mother is congratulated on the sacrifice and willingness to serve the society through carrying a new member of society. It had been found years ago that the maternal bond would be there. The goal is to diminish the bond with the child and transfer the bond to society. This serves two factors. First, the mother becomes more tied to society and the mother is more willing to release the child from her care to the care of society.

P.T. walks a balancing act. Understanding when a woman wouldn't emotionally release the tie to the baby is critical. There are those who take on a dual obligation. They keep the strong obligation to society and yet fight the Elite to keep their baby. These are reported and the

Elite deals with these quietly.
There are those who succeeded in
fighting the emotional tie to the
baby. These return to their Cast
and are given special privileges
for their willingness to serve
society. Then, there are those
who end up with a strong
attachment to the child and
weakened attachment to society.
The phrase used to describe these
among the wellness Cast was
"family first". P.T. watches
Lionia grow in attachment to her
child. The consult further
defines where Lionia is
emotionally in the process.

While doing the necessary planning
for the consult P.T. notices a
donor who watches Lionia intently.
The textbooks refer to this
attachment as the "bubble gum"
effect. When bubble gum has been
"chewed on" for awhile it became

both sticky and stretchy. The
ability to stretch out and stick
to two different objects which
aren't close together, holding
them together, is the "bubble gum"
effect. It doesn't happen often
that a donor would have this
effect. When it happens the
routine is to keep the two
separated so they don't get
"stuck" together. The Elite has
long since dismissed the idea of a
"spiritual" connection. The
society is based on serving the
society and anything "spiritual"
brings in the idea of a god
greater than society.

Chapter 9

Ayrd is a product of the society.
He was good student and trained
hard physically. With his sharp
mind and quick reflexes, he is
sent to the guard Cast. There he
excels in piloting any aircraft he
is assigned to.

The Guard Cast is responsible
for preserving the society from
outside forces. This requires
vigilance. The Guard Cast flies
over areas beyond the fence to
detect any threat to the society.
If a threat is found then the
Guard would breach the fence and
attack the threat, keeping the
society calm and secure.

Ayrd flies over areas suspected
of being inhabited by the Out
Cast. If an Out Cast threat were
spotted the location is noted and
the guard is sent to eliminate the

threat. It is troubling to Ayrd how a few Out Cast, living in the wilderness, with no army, could be a threat to the society. The fact that the Elite defines them as a threat makes them a threat.

A few months ago Ayrd detected a small group of Out Cast on one of his monthly over flights. He flew so low in his search that he could see their smiles. They actually waved their arms as if to say "Hi, glad to see you". By the time he returns from his flight and the Guard is able to get to the position, they had disappeared. If they are a threat why did they not stay to fight? Ayrd has trouble balancing the two events. Understanding is dangerous as the Elite could only allow belief of their teachings. Any questioning is not allowed.

Ayrd continued his flights. He figured out where the Out Cast might have their shelters. He flew close enough that they knew they were being watched, but far enough so he didn't find them. On every flight those smiles and the waving arms fill his memory. They had been a shock. The Casts in society don't smile. They are cautious not to give a friendly greeting. There might be an Elite recorder Cast who would determine the gesture to be forbidden. The Out Cast smiles and waves are done without fear….to their "enemy".

Ayrd studied his training. He is given the best training in fighting and flying. He keeps physically fit. Yet, he wonders how the Out Cast developed the skills to survive in the wilderness. They have to forage for their own food. They have to build their own shelters. They have to cook their own meals. They have to produce their own clothing. And they have to avoid being detected by the Elite. Ayrd thinks of the skills needed to survive in the wilderness and grows a feeling of awe toward the Out Cast. He also develops a feeling of brotherhood and trust. They had accepted him in their home even as he brought danger to them. They are experts in their lives as he is in his. Ayrd continues to study them from a distance and starts comparing their life to life in the society under the Elite. His appreciation for their way of life grows.

Other pilots talk about similar experiences. They saw the smiles and waves. They sent the Guard Cast out to find them, with no success. The difference he noted with some of the other pilots was that they see the Out Cast as too simple in mind to appreciate the society and the Elite. The Out Cast simply do not appreciate being taken care of and not having to worry about eating or shelter, or medicine, or any other . challenges of life. The pilots feel their happiness stemmed from a lack of understanding that they are in a bad situation.

Ayrd listens to these pilots. He observes that these "simple" Cast always disappear before the Guard Cast could find them. He observes that the Out Cast are able to survive the coldest winters and hottest summers. He

observes that they live with
nature and the wild animals
without fences to protect them.
He starts to wonder if the fences
were built to protect the society
from wild animals or to control
the society within the fence.

Ayrd has his routine interrupted
one Friday when he goes to his
Food Cast distribution center. He
is directed to the Child Cast
office. There he is informed that
he was chosen to be a donor. He
is given a leave of absence and
sent to the farm where he will
stay long enough to insure the
production of a healthy child.
There are facilities where he will
maintain his physical fitness. To
help him maintain his readiness
chores, growth enhancements and
regulation are designed to
maintain his fitness and keep his
skills sharp. Part of his chores

are time in the simulator. The
simulator can be set up to
simulate any airplane in the
system. He will maintain his
skills during the leave of
absence.

As the months go by Ayrd observes
that the women are given chores
that keep them from personal
contact with the men. However, he
observes their activities. Ayrd
is told that the Food Cast has
designed diets especially for the
men that are different from the
diets of the women. They don't
eat together. Ayrd notices a
difference in the women from a
distance. What is it? Is it
something in the food? Is it the
chores? Is it the comradeship
among the women? Whatever the
cause Ayrd observes a certain
"glow". There is a happiness

filling the women as they carry
their children.

One woman has such a glow that
she seems to smile. Ayrd observes
her closely. No, there is no
smile evident on her face. Yes,
there is a joy within her that
gives him a sense of a smile.
Looking at her he senses the joy
and happiness he had experienced
from the Out Cast. The feeling is
so strong that he expects her to
look at him, smile and wave.
Although they are not allowed
personal contact he begins to grow
a oneness with her. This is
something they taught in the
guard. When a pilot becomes
expert he becomes one with the
airplane. He becomes one with the
sky and the clouds. They function
as one. It is this feeling that
fills his being.

As the months go by, Ayrd is not called to donate again. The child and mother are doing well. It is a relief to think that they are doing well and that he had been fruitful. Contributing to the production of a child is understood to be like a job. It is something a person does to maintain society. Failure would mean that a person's usefulness to society is diminished. Ayrd is relieved and relaxed to know that success is in the works. He is able to enjoy his chores.

His growth regulation has minor changes. His regulation is very different than when he is at work. A Guard Cast pilot is sent on an over flight twice a month. Here he spends two hours a day in the simulator. The simulator time is logged and a record sent to his unit. This is credited to him as flight time. Additional flight time leads to promotions and benefits. It is good to be chosen by the Elite Cast for this duty.

As the months went by, Ayrd feels the essence of that woman fill his being. He wants to know what Cast she is. He wants to be able to talk to her. He wants to understand her but most of all he needs to understand the affect she is having on him. How is she able to show him a smile without smiling? How is she able to reach his inner being without even talking to him or looking at him? How is she able to invade his mind and soul without any contact? What is it about her that makes him want to know the answers? These are the thoughts that flow through his mind and keep it occupied.

It has been months since the vision of the Out Cast's smiles and waving arms interrupted his sleep or flashed across the canopy of his airplane. The last few months have been filled with a smile he has never seen and the wave that has never happened. He needs to discover the reason this exists. He feels a calmness and warmth when observing her, like he belonged with her, flying through the air, sailing on the clouds. Her presence surrounds him and flows around him and through him. It is as if she is in the simulator with him each day. The oneness he had developed as a highly skilled pilot, with his surroundings, enveloped the woman. Still, she is a distant shape on the horizon, drawing him to go there and discover the newness of the area.

Chapter 10

P.T. schedules Ayrd for a consult.
The checklist is filled out. Ayrd
had dutifully kept his chores,
even going beyond the requirements
in both his skills and his
conditioning. P.T. then went into
the emotional area. This is
always difficult. How does one
find the truth of a person's
emotions and feelings while the
barrier of contradicting the Elite
is ever present?

 P.T. proceeded like he has done
many times. How did Ayrd grow up?
What sub cell of society was his
youth spent in? When was he
chosen for the Guard Cast? How
did he perform in training
compared to his classmates? Had
he been given special missions?
Was he a good supervisor? Were
those under him skilled at their

jobs? Or were they still
progressing?

The consults slowly approached
the time at the farm. When they
got to the notice Ayrd had
received to come to the farm P.T.
noticed a change in attitude,
slightly masked. It was apparent
that Ayrd had not considered
himself a prospect to continue the
society. He was first surprised,
then had feelings there must be
some mistake. "Duty First" had
been his way of life. Now he is
called to do another "Duty" for
the Elite. Ayrd comes to the farm
still believing there is some
mistake. P.T. finds most of those
chosen feel honored and a bit
proud. Ayrd has that humility
that is rare.

P.T. finds Ayrd engaging,
honest, and able to say things in

a way that won't get him in trouble. When discussing the farm P.T. asked for his observations of the facilities. Ayrd responds that the facilities are well kept and that he is able to stay proficient. P.T. then asks for his observations of the staff. Ayrd commends the staff for their proficiency. They are "on top" of their Cast chores. At this point Ayrd goes into some detail about the efficiency of each Cast and their proficiency.

P.T. thanks Ayrd for his commendation of the staff, noting that their files will be noted and they will be honored for their proficiency. P.T. tells Ayrd, "It is rare to have a guest who is so discerning and observing. There are a few over the years who

observe objectively. A true
objective observation with points
of detail to back it up followed
with accurate discernment is
rare". Ayrd replied, "I feel it
isn't so rare, as I know others
who are trained to observe
details".

The consults were going well.
Ayrd shows a balanced disposition
and healthy psyche. P.T. then asks
Ayrd, "Have you observed the
women". Ayrd comments, "It is
difficult to understand women at
all and observing from a distance
disallows an objective
evaluation". P.T. then asks
Ayrd,"Would you help me evaluate
the women chosen to bear children
based on the physical attributes
that you observe?. Are they well
chosen? What attributes seemed to

be present in the women? What
attributes are stronger among some
of the women? Did you detect a
change in attitude from a woman's
first arrival as the months
progressed? Is there a difference
that you have noted in the
progression of certain women?"

   By this time Ayrd feels
confident that he can evaluate
objectively. "As to the first
question, I have observed the
women chosen appear to be healthy
and physically fit. These
attributes they all seem to have
in common. Although the chores
for fitness vary from person to
person each has demonstrated the
ability to do strenuous chores and
exercises requiring a high level
of flexibility.

There are differences also. Some women have a pallor to their skin when they arrive while others have been deeply tanned. I have noticed many shades in between these. Some walk smoothly as if they are on a cloud while others walk as if they are in a hurry to get where they are going. I understand these differences to be a result of their Cast and their training.

As to the second question, attributes present in a person are difficult to observe without communicating with the person. When I have observed the women talking to each other I have observed a range of openness. While we aren't allowed to be close enough to hear the conversation the facial expressions tell me that some are more involved in the communication process while others are more likely to be listeners. Those actively involved in the communication transmit a lot about their inner being as they allow it to flow more freely from the inside. Those who are good listeners have an attribute of facilitating but don't display much about their personal attributes.

As to the third question, the attribute that I observe that seemed to be stronger in the majority of the women is one of caution. Even those who talk freely stay away from substantive conversation. There is no strong reaction from any of those listening. In fact it seems that many active conversationalists barely listened to the answers or the explanation being given. In this I observe that those who simply listen have a deeper involvement in the conversation than those who appear to be actively involved but not focused on the person they were talking to.

As to the fourth question, the motions of the women progressively indicated the conversations are more about the child they are carrying as time went on. Early on, before they started showing the child's growth there is little conversation about the growth and changes. As the months went by and the time came near the conversation seemed to focus on the changes in appearance. It was interesting to note that the listeners were more likely to be more involved in conversations toward the time of birth. It seemed that they pulled together into a tighter bond getting ready for each birth.

As to the fifth question, observing from afar gives the opportunity to wonder. There are attributes hidden that can only be guessed at. There are inclinations that infer the presence of attributes that defy definition. Some women appear to be transparent, yet seem to live with depths that have not been seen or experienced. Some women appear to be as solid as a board. Closer observation detects the board floating above a sea of uncertainty. Then there is the type of woman who doesn't fit these attributes. That woman seems to be an open book: solid cover, with a depth of meaning. The story is simple, yet intriguing. The theme has a constant growth with intertwined

nuances yet, there are no
interruptions in the flow or
detours in the script.

Without knowing why, this last
type seems to encourage reading
the book in order to get to know
the story."

   P.T. thanks Ayrd for sharing his
observations. As Ayrd leaves this
consult P.T. thinks, "it has taken
me years to discover what Ayrd has
discerned in a few months, while
keeping busy with his chores. He
has been blessed with the
discovery skill. He not only is
observant, and discerning but
poetic as well. These skills have
been kept under cover in the Guard
Cast."

Chapter 11

Lionia is progressing in her consults. P.T. is working to encourage Lionia to be more open about her stress. P.T. encourages her with the results of the progress tests. Everything is normal. The baby is growing and healthy. Lionia has dodged "morning sickness". The regimen is no more stringent than what she was accustomed to before coming to the farm.

Lionia can only say that she feels something is missing. She can't tell what causes the feeling or even why she feels this way. She feels honored to help society and the Elite Cast, who has given her a good life and this opportunity. It is as if the baby isn't complete. The feeling is one of not being successful, of

not carrying a baby that has
everything. P.T. assures her that
the tests show that everything is
normal and that her concerns are
due to experiencing something new.

But "what if..?" Lionia
continues to feel and think, "what
if?" What if the baby is healthy
and the system raises her to be
unhappy? What if the baby is able
to excel and is put in a dead end
Cast? What if?

Slowly Lionia gains insight into
what is missing. "Understanding"!
She doesn't understand why the
system is so impersonal. She
doesn't understand why she has
such a strong bond with the baby.
She doesn't understand why she
needs to feel the involvement of
the donor. As a teacher she
sought to instill understanding in
her students. This made it easier

for them to accept and learn the material and their role in society. Now she is at a loss. She doesn't understand!

P.T. listens to Lionia as she searches for meaning and finds she lacked understanding. P.T. has seen this before. It happens more often than the Elite Cast would like it to happen. Lionia is drifting from her controlled environment to experience life with new meaning.

It is around this time that the session goes longer than normal. As she leaves, she almost runs into a man who is arriving for his session. A quick apology from both is uttered and Ayrd introduces himself. Lionia returns the pleasantry. Now Ayrd knows a name to go with the "person of interest". Further conversation is a violation of the rules so they continue on, Ayrd to his appointment and Lionia to her chores.

P.T. notices the exchange. His notes are brief. Nothing to cause alarm is written. A chance meeting has occurred and quickly ended. Now Ayrd is due for his consult.

P.T. starts the consult with where they had left off the previous consult, "Have you had the chance to further observe floating boards or open books? Ayrd seems to sink into deep thought, as if tying strings together to form a quilt of understanding.

He says, "With enough information, woven together properly, the most durable and workable quilt can be pieced together. First the threads, woven into fabrics, then the fabrics shaped and stitched together to form a pattern. After the pattern is stitched together the underlying batting and liner are added. Then everything is stitched together to keep everything firmly in place".

P.T. listens to the description of Lionia given as Ayrd thinks, "Lionia is a name assigned to the Teaching Cast. She is successful in searching out the core of her students to help them learn the assignments well or she wouldn't have been chosen to come to the farm. She is forthright as she looks at him directly; making eye contact, while apologizing for nearly running him over. She demonstrates the ability to trust while maintaining reserve. Her

eyes twinkled at the meet showing
a softness and warmth at the
center of her quilt. Then there
is the liner. That part that all
is stitched to, that part that is
the foundation that holds the
pieces together. The words she
used to excuse herself aren't
standard society formula. They
are personal. She has a strong
foundation."

"May I join you?" P.T. said as
he interrupted Ayrd's thoughts.
P.T. has allowed the thoughts to
progress and hopes he isn't
interrupting too soon. His timing
is carefully chosen based on the
previous meetings with Ayrd and
his understanding of how quickly
Ayrd would size up a situation.

Ayrd seems to float out of his
thoughts as an underwater swimmer
reaches for the surface to breath.

Indeed he has been holding his breath as he was trained to in meditation. The rush of air and the sound of P.T.'s voice brings him to the surface. The feeling of release is wonderful. He has a greater understanding of the enigma that has been visiting him these months. Lionia is the woman he needs to discover. Each fabric, each stitch, every angle, every shape, and the strength of her foundation needs to be learned. She is a quilt worthy of observation.

Ayrd answered "yes, the quilt has a durable fabric and has been pieced together nicely. I have seen the stitches. They are finely done by the hands of a master. The batting is soft and comforting. The backing is durable and holds the quilt together with firmness. The pieces of the quilt are varied in shape, color, and print. These need further observation to understand. The totality is….the quilt is worth caring for."

P.T. asked, "And this quilt, when did you realize its worth?"

Ayrd answered "When I arrived at the consult today".

P.T. then asked, "Was this quilt one of the books you referred to?" Ayrd answered, "A fine book with a quilt cover and a well constructed spine. It's the story that needs understanding."

P.T. changed the subject. "In your training in the Guard, how well did you do in the recon course?"

Ayrd answered, "I survived two weeks in the wilderness, until I was evacuated from the exercise."

"And why were you evacuated?"
asked P.T.

"Two weeks is the limit. Only a
few make it that long," answered
Ayrd. P.T. closes the session by
setting the next appointment a few
weeks later.

Chapter 12

Andrew and Mary are visiting
Ariean. They share their
vegetables and Ariean shares his
dried fish.

Although Andrew and Mary never
lack for wild meat, Ariean
provides meat from his cattle. On
these days they spend time
together catching up on the
movement and the welfare of the
Out Casts who are part of the
Elect.

Ariean said "the notice I have
received is that we will have
company soon. A man, woman and
young child will be joining us."

Mary asks "how young is the
child?"

Ariean responds "the child has
not yet been named".

Andrew comments, "It has been a while since we have assisted those with such a young child. What is the situation?"

Ariean then goes into what he knows, "The family is at The Farm. The father has been blessed with knowledge of his child, although he doesn't understand this yet. The mother has been blessed with the desire for family, although she doesn't know the father yet. When the time is right a Fli will send the father on a mission into the wilderness, along with the mother and child, ostensibly to test his ability to survive while caring for a woman with a child who is so young. They will travel three days without any help. On the fourth day, a scout will make contact, as before, unless they

need more time to drop their
guard. We feel that the man will
guard the camp at night and sleep
a few hours during the day. We
must be careful when making the
first contact.   The situation
will be monitored. The man has
been through rigorous training in
survival and should be able to
successfully take care of his
charges. As the situation
develops, our scout will continue
to monitor. When they have become
acquainted they will be led to
your home for hospitality. You
should have three days warning
before they arrive. A dog will be
sent when they pass the fence.
From then on you should stay close
to home in preparation."
Mary asks "Do we know their
names?"

Ariean answers "Their names are
Ayrd and Lionia."

Mary turns to Andrew and says "Lionia?"

Andrew answers "For now we must be ready. Prayers are answered in time."

On the way home Andrew and Mary are silent. Andrew has learned that a woman needs peaceful thoughts, undisturbed at times. This is one of those times. The only conversation between them is about the path, the stream to cross, the care of the food Ariean provided, and other mundane items to make the journey. The amount of food provided by Ariean is more than normal. He has mentioned that a regular delivery of milk would be forthcoming when the guests arrive. Andrew takes care of the chores, setting up camp in the evenings, breaking camp in the mornings. When Mary pitches in, he simply works with her at her pace and when she chooses to help. Normally there is a joyful bantering between the two about whom did the most work and who could get the meal faster.

This trip is different. Mary is making a retreat. Passing through the trees and the spaces, camping at night, and even sleeping, Mary is deep in prayer. This is her way. She has learned years ago to let go and depend on God for everything. It gets her through the losses and the pains of life. It gets her through the joys and happiness when she can't understand why she should even feel them. She has formed a relationship that shelters her from desiring what is not to be. She knows that asking is O.K. but demanding is wrong.

Mary knows that Andrew understands
her need. She tries to help as
before but her thoughts are not on
the journey. "Lord I have asked
that she be taken care of and that
I might see her again someday.
Today I ask that the man you have
chosen accept her and their child.
I ask you that they find a place
with us and get to know us. If
you desire, let it be known about
Andrew and me. Our journey is not
theirs. We got here by different
routes. I know that you brought
us together. Now I understand
that you are bringing them
together. Why you have chosen us
to provide hospitality and
introduce them to the skills they
will need to survive I do not
know, from my deepest being I
thank you."

Mary tries to understand the depth of what is happening. She can't fully understand why or how this is happening but turns her thoughts to what Andrew and she needs to do to get ready. There are a thousand things to consider.

She thinks, "When Andrew and I were the subjects of hospitality, our hosts simply treated us like family. There were no questions. There was no judgment for where we had been or why we ended up there. There was a family of hospitality. Yes, from the first hour we belonged. We were family! We must work to provide the same love and hospitality to Ayrd and …… Lionia."

On the journey, Andrew is thinking "When we get home we need to start getting things ready for company. The space we use for traveling guests won't do for being hosts and providing hospitality to a family with a young child. When we came here our hosts provided a home for two years. We need to make preparations for food and clothing. We need to prepare for all seasons. We need to prepare for a child to be taught and taken care of. The garden should be expanded to put up more supplies for the winter. Another deer would help us get through the winter. It will also help provide clothing. Mary will need to preserve the food and store it. A shelter will need to be made for a milk cow. There are a thousand things to do."

When Andrew and Mary arrive home they set about organizing for guests. Mary prepares the clothing and food that will be

needed. Meat is dried and
materials for clothing are
prepared. Hides and woven
materials are used for clothing
and footwear. In earlier days one
of the Elect has taught them about
mukluks. These boots have been
used for many generations in the
far north. They are very helpful
to keep feet from freezing in the
winter. When Andrew brings food
from the garden more is dried and
preserved than they would normally
keep.

Andrew immediately plants more
seeds to expand the garden and
provide more food for storage. He
sets about each day to water and
weed the garden. Then he cut down
trees and prepared them to build
walls and roofing for an addition
to the house. Time is short. It
will be faster to build three
walls adjoining their house than

to build a new four wall house.
As it is the days are long and
work is slow.

 In the society the parents are
kept at the farm until the child
is weaned. Then they are sent
back to their Casts.

There is some time to get ready
but the ever present need to have
everything ready in case a change
in plans require an earlier date
weighs on Andrew. The third week
after arriving home six men from
the area arrive to help. They had
been informed of the need by
Ariean. Mary is kept busy with
meals and water as the men work
together. The logs seem to form
themselves into well shaped walls.
The addition grows out of the
ground and the roof is finished in
a few short weeks. Andrew is able
to harvest some from the garden to

send back to their families as the newly planted garden is starting to produce.

   With the house addition finished and the helpers returning to their homes Andrew starts working on the furniture. A comfortable rocker and a bed are the first two items to be needed. Andrew works steadily on the furniture each day after tending to the garden and bringing the produce to Mary. Soon the bed and rocker are ready and Andrew starts working on the table and chairs. Cooking will be the last thing to consider as the guests will be eating with Andrew and Mary during their stay.

Chapter 13

Dan had heard phrases from the
past that seemed to make no sense,
until explained. Even then the
explanation requires an
understanding of things past.
However, they are "quaint" and
often used, even if not
understood. "The other shoe
dropped" is one of those.
Sometimes when he would get ready
for bed he would let his shoes
drop on the floor. The phrase
would come to mind and Dan would
wonder why the first shoe was not
the subject of a phrase.

Today when Dan gets to work he
found his co-worker had been given
leave, at reduced rations, and
that he had also been given leave
at reduced rations until his
machinery is fixed. Thirty days

are going to be hard. In the past
the parts to fix the machinery
only took a week. Now the parts
supply is slow. Many workers with
a thirty day leave never returned
to work. They just disappeared.
Dan headed home and thought to
himself "the other shoe dropped".

First, it is the break down. Now
it is leave with reduced rations.
The rations will be barely enough
to sustain enough energy to
survive. The requirement to go to
the food Cast distribution center
to pick up the food used more
energy than allowed for with the
reduced rations. It is as if you
are punished for equipment
failure. The Elite has their
formulas and their policies.
There is no alternative in
society. When he arrives home,

Dan finds the heat in the apartment has also been reduced. He will not be earning his quota for the next thirty days. Thankfully, Dan works outside and has warm clothing so he will be uncomfortable, but able to maintain enough warmth to survive. Rationing is a way of life. His co-worker is also an outside worker and has warm clothing. She has a fair chance at surviving the thirty days also.

The first two weeks are tough. However, Dan finds the energy to keep going. He starts to lose some weight. It is weight he can't afford to lose.

At the start of the third week, Dan arrives at the food distribution point to receive his rations. He notices his co-worker

in line also. She seems to be
weakened.

Dan hopes that the machinery will
be fixed soon so they could return
to work and have improved rations.

   On the fourth week, Dan arrives
at the food distribution point,
only to be called into the office.
He is informed that there is a
delay in the repair and no one
knows when the machinery will be
fixed. Leaving the office to get
his rations, he runs into his co-
worker. She is heading to the
office. Dan stops and introduces
himself. She responds by telling
him her name is Rani. As she
heads to the office, Dan decides
to wait for her and to accompany
her to the food distribution room.

Rani comes out of the office looking quite pale. Dan offers to accompany her to receive rations. Rani thanks Dan and is willing to hold his arm for support as they proceed to the food distribution room. Dan observes that Rani is not holding up as well as he is.

After receiving their rations Dan accompanies Rani to her apartment. He finds that she lives quite close to his apartment. After he gets back to his apartment Dan eats a small meal and sits down to figure out what to do.

It is possible that they will both be able to survive until the machinery is fixed. Dan remembers the past machinery breakdowns and that the workers seldom return. They are required to perform well and are not able to do so in a weakened condition. Thirty days

seems to be the limit of
endurance. Those workers who are
out longer than their thirty day
leave never returned. There needs
to be another option. Dan thinks
about Rani. She is a good worker
but her condition seems to be
worsening each day.

The next day is warm and sunny.
Dan sits outside to soak up the
heat. While he is relaxing and
enjoying the warmth a stranger
stops and asks Dan what he is
doing at home instead of being at
work. Dan explains that the
machinery he used had broken and
would not be fixed for a while.
The stranger asks if Dan had
plans. Dan says "I need to find a
way to survive as the rations
aren't enough to keep up my
strength. I noticed my co-worker
is getting weak faster than I am.
She is not going to be able to

return to work even if the
machinery got fixed."

The stranger mentioned, "I am in
charge of a section of the border.
I have a shortage of guards and
can use you and your co-worker, if
you are willing to re-locate".
Dan replied, "We couldn't even use
the transport to get there". The
stranger produced two transport
passes and vouchers for additional
rations to be picked up the
following week. He told Dan,
"These will get you to my section
of the border should you decide to
take up my offer".

Dan decides to accompany Rani to
the food distribution point the
following week and bring up the
subject on the walk there. If she
is willing, they will be able to
go from the food distribution

point directly to the transport
with enough food for the trip.

Chapter 14

Rani doesn't know if she will ever
make it to the food distribution
center again. She is grateful
that Dan assisted her and carried
her rations as well as letting her
lean on his arm on the walk home.
The news that the machinery is not
going to be fixed soon is a blow.
She wonders how she is going to
survive. He has reduced rations
also. She could tell he is losing
weight and getting weak.

Working in the same Cast and
living so near to each other, it
seemed impossible that they had
never met. The elite controlled
society and had kept them from
getting to know others personally.
Yesterday was a strange meeting.
Why Dan had taken the time to
introduce himself, or to accompany
her to get her rations, and then

help her get home, Rani didn't understand. She doesn't understand her feelings of gratefulness. Caring and receiving someone's help are discouraged as weakening society. Rani spends the evening going over the event and trying to understand her situation. She comes to the conclusion that survival will require working with someone else who is willing to help. Rani is willing to accept what she does not understand. She is willing to accept help from Dan.

The week is spent mostly outside during the day soaking up the heat of the sun so the rations would not be needed to provide heat during those hours. On days that it rained, Rani set out buckets to catch the rain water to supplement the water ration. It helps maintain some strength while giving her something to do to keep busy, with a minimum amount of effort.

Life has been different for Rani. When the Elite chose a Cast for each individual males were most often chosen for the Construction Cast. She doesn't know the reason she was chosen. She is petite. Had she known the story she would have known that the Elite who had named her had used the wrong name chart. The name Rani had been set aside for Construction Cast children. The fact that she had been misplaced could not be undone. She was able to learn her job and perform it well. This demonstrates that the system put in place and run by the Elite had weaknesses. While Rani was able to learn her job and perform well there are those who had had been put in a Cast who did

not perform well. These
assignments weakened society.
Rani thinks that this is quite
possibly the reason the equipment
is so slow in getting fixed.

Wrong assignments have the
possibility of shutting down the
whole system. There is a good
possibility that the some of the
Cast who make the needed parts do
not perform well and are put on
leave. The Cast that repairs the
equipment can not get the parts
and are put on leave. The Cast
that operated the machinery can't
work and are put on leave. Rani
considers that those who are put
on leave and had their rations cut
would not be able to perform
properly if called back. The
system would need to wait until
new members were trained to do the
jobs of each Cast.

It is good to have time to think. Rani had heard the phrase "through difficulties we advance". It had seemed elitist at the time. Those of the Elite Cast could humor the other Casts by convincing them that their sacrifices led to a better society.

Rani is getting another view of the phrase. It is true that this difficulty she is going through allows her to grow in her understanding of the society. Personal advancement is only encouraged as a means to further society. Rani is seeing that personal advancement as a means of fulfilling the individual was better for society.

The week pass slowly. Rani makes sure to stretch her rations out so she has food each day. This is the best way to keep

going. She also spends time
asking for help. She would think
"please send someone to fix the
equipment or even find a way to
provide adequate rations until the
equipment is fixed." Those
thoughts are aimed at the
universe. There must be someone
or somehow the message would be
heard and answered. Rani needs to
continue to hope. She realizes
that hopelessness would cause her
to give up and stop eating.
"Please help me survive this
ordeal" she would say. Surely her
thoughts are heard or understood
by someone.

It was again time to walk to the
food distribution point. She
needed to start early as she is
moving more slowly now. She
needed to stop often to rest.

Rani packs up her clean containers and is preparing to get started when she hears a knock at the door.

Chapter 15

Dan is moving slower now. He knows that Rani will also be moving more slowly. Today is the day they will go to the food distribution point and pick up their rations. Dan starts early so they will have enough time to make it to the center. He remembers to put the vouchers in his pocket. He also carefully wraps some utensils and places them in his pocket. The voucher for the transport is carefully put in another pocket. He picks up the clean dishes and starts out.

It doesn't take too long to get to Rani's and Dan knocks on her door. When Rani opens the door he notices that she has her dishes and is heading out. Dan says, "May I carry your dishes for you?". She gratefully hands them

to him. He offers her his arm and
they start out together.

   The walk is slow and they often
stop for a rest. On the journey
Dan explain how the visitor has
offered them a position on the
border and given them vouchers for
extra food and transportation.
Dan tells her the plan is to pick
up their rations and go from there
to the transport. This will
reduce the amount of walking and
better utilize the energy they
have. They will eat some of the
rations on the way to the
transport and will be able to
relax and reenergize a bit on the
trip. They can also eat a bit on
the transport.

   When they arrive at the food
distribution point, they are
called into the office and

notified, "You are being sent to the border to take a position there. The Elite have seen it necessary to fill those positions and you have been chosen. Here are passes that validate the change in Cast. New clothing issue will be waiting for you when you arrive at your new location. Draw their rations and proceed as soon as possible to your new job".

 Dan and Rani feel a weight lift off their shoulders. This makes it official and they will be all right. They proceed to the ration room, turn in their dishes and draw their rations. With the transfer there is no question about the extra rations. Dan and Rani then walk to the transport station. There they wait for a few hours until their transport

comes. They find a quiet place
and share a meal together. Rani
thinks, "Thank you" to whoever had
answered her petition and helped
Dan and herself have a way to
survive. Then she thinks, "Thank
you" for the extra rations, and
"Thank you" for sending Dan to
help her.

Dan notices Rani is very quiet and
sees almost asleep as he retrieves
the utensils from his pocket and
opens a tray so they can eat.
Just as the food is ready, Rani
opens her eyes and comes alive.
Her eyes flash with life and her
smile brings warmth to Dan's
heart. It feels good to help a
co-worker. They quietly eat the
meal without conversation. Their
actions of passing food to one
another and making sure the other
one was taken care of are full of
meaning. The actions say, "I care

137

about you" and, "I want you to be strong again". At this time words would not have had the depth of meaning that the actions have.

After they eat, Dan carefully packs the food and empty tray and prepares to board the transport when it arrived. When the transport arrives, they quickly board and find some comfortable seats for the journey. It is late afternoon and the transport has been carrying workers home from work. Many of them have already been let off so the transport is almost empty. It continues throughout the night to the border.

Rani and Dan sleep for much of the journey. When they awake the dawn is just lighting the sky. They open their food container,

removing a meal, and eat once
again. The scenery passing by
becomes brighter and more intense
as the sun rises. They pass areas
where food is grown. Some of the
crops are in bloom and the colors
make the world seem alive with
life. They will be at their
destination soon.

Chapter 16

  P.T. is thinking, "The weeks
have passed and it is time to
start putting the puzzle together.
Lionia is due to deliver and I
have been notified that two others
will be arriving at the border.
They will need a guide who is
strong enough to carry more than
his share. The pieces are all
there. The timing is important,
although the others will do well
to spend time at the border
gaining strength while learning
survival skills".

P.T. arranges for Ayrd and Lionia
to have consultations around the
same time. There is a scheduling
"mistake" that causes them to both
be in the waiting room for a while
before the first appointment.

P.T. has been "delayed" by an urgent meeting. This delays the consult further.

Ayrd arrives for his consult and is notified that P.T. has been delayed. Ayrd will need to wait in the waiting room until P.T. is available. It shouldn't be too long. As Ayrd enters the waiting room he finds the woman for whom he had searched to understand. She is reading a book on education and evidently waiting patiently for her delayed consult.

Ayrd notices that she has a bit of discomfort and asks, "is there is something I can do to help you be comfortable while you wait". After all, he was informed that his consult is second in line and she is the only other one waiting. She would go first. Lionia looked

up, smiled, and said, "Thank you
for your concern. In time, the
discomfort will pass. It is just
something that comes with the
task".

"My name is Ayrd. We have a bit
of time. Would you feel
comfortable telling me about
yourself?"

 Lionia responded, "Like what?"

Ayrd breaks into a grin and says,
"You could start with your name
and then expound on your training
and Cast. When you have justly
explored the echoes of your past
you could delve into the desires
of your future. I am a good
listener."

Lionia paused, looked deeply into
his eyes and sensed that this
"Ayrd" was a mixture of Bard and
assurance. She felt she could

trust this man who had an honest
look and poetic flow. Lionia
started with, "My name is Lionia.
Like all children in society I was
raised by the system, apart from
my parents. I did have an
extraordinary beginning as my
parents conceived me outside the
Farm and were able to raise me for
a couple of years before they were
discovered. At that point I was
taken to the society schools and I
lost track of them. My studies of
the society have taught me that
they were probably convicted by
the Black Robes as being in the
movement and were sentenced as Out
Cast. They were probably unable
to survive in society. I hope
they found a way to survive. I do
have a faint memory of them,
teaching me and training me,
before I was taken away.

My schooling went quickly as I had a better start than the others at my level. As a result I finished several years ahead of my age group and began teaching at quite a young age. When I would get tired of studying and want a break, the word "focus" would flash from my memory to my mind. That word had been ingrained in me at a very young age. In that word, my mother was with me through my studies. She helped me succeed from the past. My parents also taught me that we are given bodies to take care of. Nutrition and exercise are necessary components of living a good life. I didn't think about their teaching much as the years went by. I just learned to use exercise to keep my body working at an optimum level. This was noted in my progress reports over the years. I believe that the Elite who review the reports and pick those to come to the farm made the decision to send me based on the overall conditioning I have received.

I arrived at the Farm and have followed the schedule prepared for me. The baby is doing well and I have been told the father is a strong, healthy, and bright man. He was chosen specifically because of the common traits found with my file. I understand he has a sharp mind which has shown itself to be both introspective and analytical. I have felt his presence growing within me. The baby is meant to be an asset to society."

She pauses. Ayrd interrupts. "And what are the desires of your future?"

Lionia pauses and thinks about the consequences of sharing her dream to an Elite or a spy. She feels she can trust Ayrd. "I have been taught to work for the good of society and I think we should all do our best to improve society. Looking back to my youth and the beginning my parents gave me, it might be good if the elite allowed me to raise this child for at least a couple of years. We want the best for society and I wonder if a child, raised by a mother and a father, isn't a greater asset to society. However, I need to return to teaching and will be unable to care for the child. There is no father to help raise the child. If there were the elite would not allow it. Still, I do wonder which is really best. Maybe the

Elite will someday change the rules."

At this point Lionia is called for her consult with P.T. As she leaves, she turns to Ayrd and says, "Ayrd, you are a good listener. I hope I haven't bored you. Thank you for listening." Lionia then proceeded to the consult room.

Ayrd mused the content of what he had just experienced. It would be inaccurate to say "what he had heard" as the wording was just a part of what she had communicated. There is a depth of caring and love that he had not experienced in society. Ayrd remembers the Out Casts smiles as he flew the recon patrols. It is hard to understand the fear of the elite that the Out Cast would attack. They are so scattered and discouraged that the idea is far-fetched. However, the opportunity to fly and keep up his skills is always welcomed. What is it about this woman called Lionia and the Out Cast he has become "acquainted" with? Is it love? Is it openness? Is it the idea of "family"?

Her consult starts before she had the chance to ask him about himself. Ayrd feels a sense of relief. He wants to focus on her and that would be a distraction. The other pilots and the trainers trusted and liked Ayrd. When asked to describe him there is little they really knew. He is adept at being a good listener. Few even think of asking him about his background. When he is through listening they feel they have known him from the beginning. In fact, he is never really

through listening. Their every
day challenges are always of
interest. Ayrd cares about those
he works with.

Ayrd's thoughts shift. For the
first time in memory, he met
someone he wants to share his life
with. He would enjoy describing
his childhood and education. He
would enjoy sharing the thrills
and expectations in the Guard Cast
with her. But first, he intends
to get to know all about her.

Chapter 17

Andrew works to be ready for
guests. Although two of them will
be under tutelage there are now
two more that will be passing
through. Andrew prepares to go to
another homestead and help prepare
living quarters there.

 He remembers the time before.
The society allowed freedom to
choose and freedom to move and
work and play. Slowly, over a
period of almost 100 years, they
taught generations to rely on the
Elite Cast to take care of them.
The Elite Cast would slowly "take
care" of one more part of life
each cycle until they had complete
control and those freedoms were
lost. A few had conserved the
history and passed it down to
their associates and family. When
they were caught they were taken

to the border and sent to the
wilderness to die at the face of
wild animals.

Andrew thinks about all of this as
he helps construct an abode for
the other two. They are taught
that separate living quarters will
be needed. Although, a common area
will be useful until they recover
their strength and can begin to
help each other more and not rely
on the others as much.

The quarters are quickly finished.
The basic furniture is all that
was left. Andrew will construct
one piece at home and bring it
later. Others will each construct
a piece.

Andrew arrive home to find that
Mary has tended the garden,
harvested produce, and had been
drying and canning the food for
storage. He set about helping her

during the day while spending
evenings working on the furniture.
The days fly by and the evenings
are busy. Andrew and Mary never
discuss their thoughts yet each
think of "Lionia" and wonder.
Maybe, just maybe…. The guest
house is solid and can be a
permanent residence. Normally, the
new Out Casts could learn
sufficiency and relocate to their
own location. The house Andrew
built, was more than needed for a
short term stay. In the back of
his mind there is hope. Maybe
there will be a more permanent
need.

Fall is soon approaching. The
package from the seed bank arrives
for a fall garden. As the summer
produce is harvested room is made
for a cool weather planting. They

were well located. They are near
a stream where water is readily
available for irrigating. Their
dwelling is above the mark that
would be touched by even a flash
flood. An irrigation pipe ran
from upstream that carried water
to the house for washing and
watering. Normally, drinking
water came from the rain barrels.
When this ran short the stream
water pipes had a diversion to a
charcoal and sand filter system.
This helps insure safe drinking
water.

Into the hillside, away from
their home, a storage room was
built. It is fairly large when
the side rooms were taken into
consideration. The front had an
entrance four feet deep as the
front walls are four feet thick.
The side rooms had separate
entrances and are cold rooms. In

the winter they are either filled
with packed snow or frozen ice
from the river. They had drainage
for melting ice and snow to
escape. Once they were filled and
the door was closed they kept the
central storage room cold the
entire summer. The central
storage room is large enough for
two hanging deer or cattle along
with racks for vegetables and
fruits. A separate "cave" has
been constructed that they called
a "potato cellar". This simply is
deep enough that the temperature
stays 54 degrees Fahrenheit year
round. It is for storing produce
that will be harmed if frozen.

Chapter 18

Rani and Dan arrive just short of noon at their destination. They are met by Schort. Schort assists them into a conveyance and carries them through check points to their destination.

Schort is of the Employment Cast. His job is to help get relocated and settled in a different location or new Cast (a rare event). Although Schort is of the Employment Cast he is also a Fli and will help Rani and Dan to resettle. If everything goes well they will resettle with the Out Cast and begin a new life. Today, they will be given housing and food. Tomorrow, they will be outfitted with new uniforms and begin their training. Schort will explain that the training will be for skills that are necessary yet

are seldom used in society. There
are few chosen for this training.
Rani and Dan will be the only
students in the class. Tonight,
they will begin the road to
getting their strength back. The
quarters are warm. The food is
sufficient. The service was
unexpected. A maid and a cook
were assigned. Their job is to
teach Rani and Dan to clean and to
cook. This is the first road to
self sufficiency. It is also
these basic skills that can be
worked on while they grow
stronger.

Rani and Dan, thankful for the
help, gladly set out to learn.
The foods are foreign and the
cooking utensils are like they had
never seen. The food is not prepackaged or pre-cooked. It is raw
and unprocessed. They need to
learn to preserve it and to use a

variety of foods to create
balanced menus. There isn't a lot
of time. A few months and they
are scheduled to leave. The
training starts slow at first,
covering the basics. Then, as
they get stronger, the pace picks
up and becomes more involved.

What Rani and Dan do not find out
until much later is that Schort
brought them to an area outside
the fence. They have left the
comforts of society. The fresh
food is supplied by the Out Cast.
The training is supplied by the
Out Cast. The training center is
outfitted close to society and
seems to be a group of empty
buildings, preserved so those
inside could look from the fence
and observe how bad things had
been before the Elite had taken
control of the society. Somehow
the buildings were out of sight of

those in society and the few at
the border ever saw them. There
was a purpose to keeping them up,
so the Elite Cast could hold them
up as a failed monument to a
failed system. It must have been
a Fli that sold them on the idea,
as these buildings are ideal for
their present use. They are a
good training center which is out
of sight and any use is not
noticed. When people are noticed
around the buildings it is easy to
explain that an upkeep crew is
taking care of them. The buildings
couldn't be approached without
going outside the fence so
verification is not possible.

Rani and Dan soon regain their
strength and continue learning
survival skills like the citizens
of old had learned. Although
those of old learned over a
lifetime and were very proficient

Rani and Dan are gaining basic
skills that, with help, they could
build on.

Dan is introduced to tools he had
heard about. These are tools that
the society no longer feel they
need. Dan soon realizes that an
operator of equipment could repair
many of the small breakdowns with
such tools. This would keep the
machines working and increase
production. The Repair Cast are
the only ones allowed to do any
repairs and they are limited to
the tool supplied and the parts
supplied. This comes from the
idea fostered in the past society
that each worker is not to do the
job of another worker for fear of
that worker not being needed and
losing that job. It led to
inefficiencies, but society is set

up this way and suggestions to the contrary are not kindly accepted by the chosen one.

All changes and schedules have to be approved by the Chosen One, even the change in Cast. Rani and Dan thought this change in their lives was done by the Chosen One. The truth remains much more intricate than that. In a past society, forged documents were used to enter a society. Their documents were forged for them to be able to leave the society.

Rani is even more enthused by the tools. These would be able to allow someone like her (petite), to be able to do repairs also. Working with the tools as they are taught is a wonderful experience. Rani remembers hearing the phrase "like Christmas" and wondering what it means. Now she feels that this is "like Christmas".

The training continues and they both become stronger and more proficient with basic tools. They also become able to do basic chores like cleaning and cooking. These chores include using clean water and "field sanitation" (basic survival outdoors).

In the field sanitation course, they are outfitted with different clothes. Their shoes give way to a sturdy boot. Their Cast clothes are heavier and made for durability. They spend days away from the buildings learning land navigation and the art of hiking rough terrain. Rani and Dan grew up learning not to question authority so they apply themselves without questioning the skills

they are learning. They are happy
to have food and have regained
their strength. They are happy to
be learning new things.

Chapter 19

P.T. helps Lionia get comfortable. He asks her, "How are you doing? What has the Medical Cast told you about your "time"?. Lionia tells him, "I am doing quite well. The discomfort is to be expected. I am looking forward to delivering the baby".

P.T. asks, "what are your feelings toward the baby?". Lionia replies, "I feel the baby will be an asset to the society. I feel that it will be healthy and strong as I have been given the best care for health and nutrition. The chores are beneficial and the regimen is well planned for a successful addition to the society".

P.T. asks, "Are you prepared for the next phase, that of nurturing the baby until the time comes to

move the Citizen to the Nurturing
Cast?". She responds "I am
indeed, looking forward to the
nurturing phase". At this time,
P.T. detects an above average
excitement. Lionia is, indeed,
very involved with her child.
P.T. explains, "You will need to
go through a period of physical
training during this phase so that
your body will fully recover and
regain the strength you are using
for the baby. This training will
be planned for you while taking
into consideration your personal
traits and abilities. Help will
be provided to get you through the
tougher parts".

Lionia leaves the consult with
thoughts swimming through her
mind. The idea of continuing
chores during the nutrition stage
hadn't occurred to her. It makes
sense. The society is thinking of

her as well as the baby. What was
it that P.T. had said, "Citizen?"
That is odd. All members of
society are referred to as such…
Members! There is something to
this that she does not fully
understand.

For now, it is good to know that
the Chosen One and the Elite Cast
have her best interests in mind.
She will do her part to produce a
valuable member of society and get
back in shape so that she can
return to teaching.

P.T. calls Ayrd for his consult.
P.T. notifies him that the time is
getting closer for him to return
to his Guard Cast. P.T. estimates
about three to four months is the
longest Ayrd will need to be here.
P.T. told Ayrd, "Recovery after
child birth sometimes tasks a
while. There is a woman who is

being programmed to undergo a period of rigorous physical training during that time. The skills you have been taught and become quite proficient at can be used to help her learn and regain her strength. There will be challenges in terrain navigation, exercises to increase endurance, problem solving situations, and hard decisions required during the exercise. At the same time, she will be required to protect and nurture her child".

P.T. continued, "I have seen nothing like this in my past training records, but your file is filled with notations on your ability to problem solve quickly and efficiently with those under your care at the top of "the list." Your success in the recon course indicates that you would likely be able to handle these conditions. This makes you a prime candidate for this exercise. And one last thing. This exercise is to be totally voluntary for you. If you choose not to do it, another guide will be chosen."

"It is possible," P.T. continued, "that you may not return from this exercise. If that is the case, your position in the guard will be filled. The decision to fill your position will not be made by the Elite Cast until they have received notification that you will not return. That will be taken care of for you as your success in the exercise will be closely monitored."

P.T. moved on to Ayrd's changes during the past nine months. "Did you have further observations or insights on the quilt? The story that needs understanding?"

Ayrd answered, "I have been able to further delve into the mystery of the quilt. The fabric seems to be substantial. The stitching is done with much care early on and continued to pull the pieces together over time. Somewhere I read of a star quilt that was pieced together and given as a gift. This quilt is a star quilt of the finest fabrics and stitching. This quilt is being quite a gift to all who have the opportunity to experience the gift. The colors are vibrant and the pattern attracts a certain feeling of comfort and understanding. It is a quilt that one would want to possess. Still, it is a quilt that can not be owned, just cared for and kept safe. In this way all who experience the quilt can experience the gift." Ayrd continued, "The star quilt, as the story goes, was a special gift, meant to bring into the home the love and caring of the quilter. It symbolizes a feeling of family as the culture is one of extended families who care for one another. The hours of labor in creating the quilt is the real gift. It means that someone is willing to spend time and labor to have something to share. It means that the giver is a sharing person. That culture has a lot of focus on sharing as the attribute is needed to survive. Food is often scarce. Those who have would share. Shelter is hard to acquire. Those who have shelter helped those who didn't. This attribute helps that society survive. There is a rumor that society may even survive today somewhere. I believe that is possible as I have found the

ability to help each other
strengthens each person."

P.T. then asked Ayrd, "Could you
make a correlation between the
quilt and the woman you had met in
the waiting room?". Ayrd seems to
sink into deep thought. In fact,
he is mentally sketching his
response. The response must be
both accurate and acceptable by
the standards of the Elite. If he
demonstrates affection, it would
hurt his career in the Guard Cast.
If he demonstrates negativity
toward another Cast, it would also
hurt his career in the Guard Cast.
Ayrd had a solid position
primarily because he learned to
encourage others to do the
talking. He learned a lot about
them. At the same time, he had
not risked offering opinions that
could be misconstrued. Now, a
representative of the Elite is

asking him for an observation. It would be good to keep the answer focused on the quilt and not personalize it if possible. Ayrd answered, "In the few minutes that I was in her company in the waiting room, I observed that she seems to be similar to the quilt. She seems to be one of the best of her Cast. In addition to that, she seems to have the upbringing and training that help her become a versatile and proficient teacher. On reflection, I could say the training and growth she had is indeed like the pieces and stitching of the quilt. Her students would be motivated to learn by her presentation. This is like the colors of the quilt that brighten the room. As to the story of the quilt, I mentioned that each quilt presents its own story. Like the quilt she has her

own life story. Indeed, Society
has given her students a gift."

    P.T. indicated, "The consult is
over for the day, consider helping
with the training exercise, and
let me know within a week as
preparations will need to be
made".

Chapter 20

Ariean kept busy making
preparations. The word arrived
that there will be five sent into
the exercise. The exercise is to
last two weeks. That means that
supplies have to be pre-positioned
in order to support the exercise.
Ariean has been receiving food
from the Out Casts. He packages
the food so that it can be pre-
positioned where animals can not
get into it. It also has to be
pre-positioned where it can be
retrieved easily, depending on the
route the five end up taking. The
leader of the five has a
reputation for irregular routes
that can not easily be followed or
pre-determined.

The guides are informed and their
dogs are ready. This exercise
requires the guide and his dog to

work as one, constantly
communicating with each other
while remaining silent and living
in the shadows. It will be the
responsibility of the dog to
follow the scent and stay behind,
where the scent would start
getting old. This will help
maintain the secrecy needed. The
guide will be constantly observing
the terrain so that they will pass
through open areas that are not
visible from the distance. He
will always be aware that the
leader will double back and check
his back trail. Even a trail with
an "old scent" can be observed by
a good guide. This is often
addressed by a guide using two
dogs. One will follow closer and
return to notify the guide when
the path changed. The other will
stay with the guide. The guards
had been taught to survive in the

wilderness and protect themselves from wild animals. The idea of trained dogs had not been in their training. Seeing a "wild" dog, if one of the guide dogs were ever spotted, will only make the guard stay alert for the need for safety actions.

Ariean calls a meeting of the guides and points out the locations of the pre-positioned supplies. Along with food there is a supply of dry wood so the food can be cooked without smoke. A camp stove has been constructed and stationed at each location. The stove has a diffuser that will be installed over the fire and scatter any smoke that does arise. There is also a sleeve that surrounded the fire to keep the light from being seen. It also protects the fire from wind.

The guides have to be prepared whether the exercise brings them toward the homes of the Out Cast or into the desert areas. Because there will be a new mother and baby with them the likelihood of the desert areas is less. Early contact is not to be attempted. They would only provide food and water when the success of the exercise required it. This will probably be after the fourth day. The guides will have to make that determination at the time. If the exercise is in danger of outpacing the pre-positioned resources the guides will send a dog to Ariean for further support.

In the past there are those referred to as "Native Americans". They prided themselves in counting coup. One of the bravest deeds, earning many coup, was to be close enough to the enemy to touch the clothing or to remove a part of his clothing or tools in his possession without being noticed. This skill has been ingrained in the guides. They have learned the art of being present without being seen. Sometimes they will stay in a position, without moving, for hours at a time. Some will do so an entire day and only move at night. Although these guides have skills beyond most of the Out Cast they are treated as part of the family with no special treatment. This is the strength of the Out Cast, their acceptance of each other's skills with equality.

The guides are informed that the leader of this exercise will be a challenge for even the best guide. Precautions will need to be made at every step as the leader has been well trained and has been observed in the past when he

completed an exercise outside the
society in training. This one is
one of the best. No
misunderstanding can be allowed.
The success of the exercise
depends on everything happening as
planned.

Chapter 21

Schort sits down with Dan and
Rani. "You have made good
progress. The basic skills you
have been taught will be helpful
in the future. We need to get you
ready for the next step. An
exercise has been planned to help
you further your skills and gain
more strength. It will be a tough
exercise, with challenges you have
never dreamed of and the
opportunity to achieve things you
never believed you could. There
will be five of you going on the
exercise. You will be provided
with a leader who has skills that
you will need to complete the
exercise. With the grace of God
you will be successful."

Schort continued, "In preparation
for the exercise, the next week or
two we will be making short

training outings where we will carry food and provisions into the wilderness and return after a few days."

The next morning an outfitter was there when they awakened. She measured and fitted backpacks for both of them. Schort already had his backpack, which looked well used. She showed them the basic provisions they would need and how to pack them into the back packs to reduce the stress on their bodies.

The next day Schort had supplies laid out for them. After they packed the outfitter and Schort led them into the wilderness for an over night outing. The trip was uneventful and they returned the next day, tired from carrying the supplies out, and the long trip back. Two days later they packed enough for four days: two days out and two days back. Another rest period of two days and they packed again, this time for three days out and three days back. They were never far from the buildings as their route actually circled around.

After two weeks of preparation they are starting to get used to the pack and have learned the need to load the pack properly. They will be packing enough to go for two weeks without re-supply.

Schort sat them down again. "You have felt muscles you didn't know you had. You should be getting them worked out by now. The last trip should have been easier and less tiring." He reviewed with

them what they had observed and
what their ideas were about the
observations. They had both
noticed the absence of transports
and buildings. The hum of
machinery is missing and the
sounds of the nights are very
different. Aside from that, the
change in their ability to carry
the packs and camp under the skies
is both noticed and accepted with
a certain pride of achievement.

Chapter 22

Lionia delivers a baby boy and names him Andy. That will be his name until the Elite Cast decides what the need is and what Cast they decided he belongs in. A name within the Cast list will then be bestowed upon him. Lionia will be able to resume her normal routine in a week or so. She will only stay at the farm until Andy is weaned and can go to the Education Cast.

Two weeks later, her chores include a consult with P.T. At this consult, P.T. asks her, "How is your recovery going?". She replies, "I am ready to return to my school whenever the Elite Cast decides I am ready to go". P.T. asks her, "Has your stay at the farm gone well?". She replies,

"it was a great break, but I am
ready to resume work as soon as
requested."

P.T. informed her, "There is an
exercise that you are to undertake
to determine your fitness to
return to work. It will be
programmed in two weeks and the
exercise will test your endurance
and fitness. Meanwhile, you are
to keep your exercises up and
check with the Medical Cast if
anything comes up that would cause
you not to have a full recovery".

 P.T. scheduled the next consult
for a week later.

After Lionia left P.T., Ayrd came
in for his consult. P.T. asked
him, "Have you considered the
exercise?" Ayrd responded, "I
agree to the exercise". P.T. then

spelled out the exercise, "There will be five, including you. One will be a child. Care must be taken to protect the child and mother as well as the other two. They will be sent into the wilderness with provisions for two weeks. It will be up to you to provide for the group. You can expect to meet trials, dangers, and some pleasant parts of the journey. Provisions for success will be sent with you. You will be able to hunt and gather along the way. Providing and preparation will be your job. The other parties will only be introduced to you the day they start on the journey and the journey will be classified, so this information can not be shared with anyone".

"Do you understand?" P.T. asked.

Ayrd replied, "I understand that this is to be kept to myself. Have the other parties been notified yet?"

P.T. answered, "They are being notified as needed".

Ayrd returned to his quarters and started his mental planning. "Wilderness journeys are not for the faint hearted or weak. Movement will be slowed with a woman and child so the distance covered in two weeks will be less than I would plan for myself. It would go better if I had a special carrier for the child and the woman can carry the child part time and I can carry the child part time. By trading off every hour or two the task will be easier and they can go further each day.

I would have to change my chores to include weight training to be in his best shape when they start. I would request special packs and loads so I could get used to the expected weight and load distribution. A young child might only add six to ten pounds but every ounce will make a difference in the exercise. Each adult will need to carry their share of the provisions. As the food is consumed the weight will lessen. By the end of the first week the total weight I will be carrying, with the child, will be about equal to the beginning weight without the child. At that time, the difference will be weight distribution and mobility.

If there should be a situation facing wild animals or dangerous trails my reaction time will be impeded. Traveling in the open as much as possible will allow for an earlier warning as I will be able to see things developing at a distance. I hope I can train one of the others to watch the back trail every few minutes. That will allow me to watch the trail and only have to check the back trail every ten minutes or so. A view of where we have walked will be important should there be a need to retrace the trail. Landmarks look different from each angle.

In a previous exercise, I had been able to cover over thirty miles in a day. This had been with minimal weight and dehydrated foods. I always camped near water and made sure to carry enough water for the day. Although the water alone added almost ten pounds it was distributed in a special backpack. I had not

needed items for personal
cleaning. This time these items
will be needed. A woman along
will require certain etiquette.

Twelve to fifteen miles the first
day will be enough. Fifteen to
twenty miles the second day will
be enough. Twenty to twenty five
miles a day the rest of the trip
will be enough. In fourteen days
I will plan to cover around 270
miles. The rest of the trip will
depend on the ability to gather
food.

 I will need to plan the menus for
the trip. P.T. will provide the
food and gear needed. He needs to
prepare a list. Three adults and
a child require different
preparation than himself alone. I
have to be prepared within days.
While keeping up my chores I will
need to coordinate with P.T. to

gather the supplies needed and
position them for the journey."

Chapter 23

Dan and Rani are completing their preparations for the exercise. Schort calls them into the dining room for a briefing and a relaxing lunch. "The exercise you have been preparing for includes three others. The woman joining you has a young baby. This will make the exercise more difficult and require everyone to work together and do more than you have needed to do thus far. The man joining you has been chosen as he has the skills to give you the best chance of success. He will be in charge. If you are to complete the exercise you will need to learn from him and work as closely with him as you can."

Schort continued, "The exercise will start within a few days. The items you have been practicing with may change as the items you will take will be chosen for their need to complete the exercise and keep the weight as light as possible. Remember to pay attention to his guidance and feel free to share with him how you are doing at any time. The exercise is to go longer than two weeks. You will have provisions for two weeks. After that your food will need to be provided from the land." Schort then left to do some coordinating.

Dan and Rani discuss the situation. It has been a real blessing for them to be here. They have been able to have food and exercises. They recovered their strength and gained in physical fitness. The exercises they had gone on brought them to the point that they are confident that they can complete the new exercise.

Their conversation turns to the prospect of having a baby on the exercise. A baby could cry and traveling quietly will be out of the question. The time needed to take care of the baby may be a blessing. Frequent stops will help them also. The mother will be challenged with carrying the baby as well as her share of the provisions. Dan would offer to carry the baby at times. Rani is also willing, but doesn't have the size or weight needed for the extra load. Dan tells Rani, "I can do that part and you can help in other ways. At the camp sites, you can help with the baby and the cooking. There will be plenty to do at the end of each day. The mother will be tired and help then will be appreciated".

The discussion then turned to the prospect of the man who would be in charge. Where did he acquire his skills? What Cast would have trained a man in the skills necessary to survive in the wilderness? Why does this exercise include them along with the other three? These are questions that they can not answer. They need to trust Schort. So far he has done everything necessary to help them survive. The question that goes unspoken is "what Cast are they being prepared for?" There are some things that they will have to wait to find out.

The supplies start arriving. Rani and Dan start checking them out based on a check list provided to

them. The task takes some time.
They need to verify that every
item is accounted for as the
supplies arrive. A packing list
is also provided. There will be
four packs. Items are separated
and laid out next to each pack.
The food items will be added at
the last minute. Which personal
items are allowed will be added at
the last minute also.

Chapter 24

Andrew and Mary are close to being
ready. Ariean informs them, "The
needed food has been supplied and
is being prepared. Some of it has
to be dried. Some has to be
smoked. Some has to be canned.
He estimates that they are 80%
finished with the preparation.
The initial food packets are
already being positioned. Since
the first packet is intended to be
accessed after those on the
exercise had been journeying for
two weeks, the remaining packets
will be ready and positioned
before they are needed.

Andrew and Mary are starting to
harvest the second crop.
Vegetables are being prepared and
stored for supporting the
sojourners for several months.
Meanwhile, each day there is time

spent in prayer. With the
exercise ahead there will be
trials and dangers that will need
to be encountered and overcome.
They have found that prayer is
answered. The safety of the
sojourners is the focus of their
prayer.

It is a slow change. First, the
Black Robes ruled that prayer in
the schools and public is
unlawful. They then ruled that
all prayer is to be confined to
the churches. This was accepted
as those who prayed chose not to
offend others. Then the Black
Robes ruled that prayer at home is
unlawful. This is to keep
visitors from being offended and
keeps the children from being,
"indoctrinated". The schools are
changed to teach the children the
"truth" of the society and to
gather information about the

actions of the parents. By the
time the children are two they are
taken to the Nurturing Cast.
There they start their education.

By this time the laws had been set
and it was too late to challenge
them. Then the churches closed.
The Black Robes determined that
productivity is being harmed by
those who chose to go to church
instead of working. This is bad
for society and was stopped. Some
of the churches are turned into
training centers. Others are
turned into food distribution
centers or storage houses. All of
the needs an individual would have
are provided by the state.

At first this seems to work well
as those with assets and an income
are simply taxed to care for those
without assets and an income. The
incentive to work in order to

build something is lost. The
initiative to develop new things
and bring them to market is
diluted as the development is only
for the state. New items are
automatically a possession of the
state. Those ideas that are not
fully developed (as all items are,
until they are tested and refined)
are taken by the state to be
developed. The Development Cast
do not have the vision of the
inventor. The end product often
does not work or brakes down
easily when it does work.
Productivity vanishes. Those
working lose the will to work and
joined those who are taken care
of.

The state determined that the
problem is wealth. Money is
abolished. Property is taken by
the state. All were assigned to
Casts and are expected to

contribute. They are taken care
of as the Elite Cast determines
their need.

Chapter 25

Lionia has given birth to a boy
child. The term "mother" has been
taught in reference to animals but
human women are called "carriers"
as their job is to "carry" the
child until born and weaned, then
to hand the child over to the
nurturing Cast. Lionia holds her
child and the word "mother" fills
her being. A mother is more than
an animal giving birth. A mother
has a connection with the child
that reaches beyond understanding.
Lionia feels the connection.
Lionia is immersed in motherhood.
She has seen the result of the
children she taught who had no
mother or father. She wants a
better future for her son. A
month has passed and the time for
leaving is only a couple of months
away. Lionia thinks. "What might

be if my son has a real father …
real parents to raise him".

Ayrd completes his planning and is
waiting for P.T. to "pull the
cord". This is a term they use
meaning to begin the descent to
safety. It comes from using a
parachute and falling to the
earth. It has also become the
phrase for beginning a task. P.T.
has informed him that, "The child
has been born. You will go on the
exercise as soon as the mother is
ready". Ayrd saw Lionia and her
son in passing and the eyes of the
young boy seems to fix on his own.
There is something about the boy
that is familiar. Ayrd fights
against the desire for this woman
and child to be the ones he is to
take on the exercise. He has a
deep desire for them to be the

ones but knows that he will have
to focus on those who are already
chosen and not be distracted by
this woman and child. Still,
there is something strong within
his being that attracts him to
them as a magnet.

P.T. calls Ayrd in for a consult.
"It is time to put the exercise
into action. You will have a
change of clothes ready and will
need to be changed and at the
perimeter of the farm at midnight.
You will be met there by the
mother and child. You will leave
immediately and be taken to a
place where you will be outfitted
with the supplies needed to
undertake the journey. Two days
will be allocated for preparation
and rest before the four will
begin the trek. The other two are

already at the place and have been
prepared for the exercise."

At midnight, Ayrd is waiting at
the perimeter location where a
conveyance is waiting. A man who
introduces himself as Schort is
the driver. Within minutes Lionia
and the boy appear. Schort helps
them board the conveyance. Once
they are settled he carries them
off to the meeting place. Ayrd is
both filled with joy that Lionia
and the boy are the ones chosen
for the exercise and feels a sense
of responsibility for their safety
that is stronger than he normally
feels.

When they arrive, Ayrd and Lionia
are taken to their rooms and
instructed to get some rest.
Tomorrow will be a long day.

Chapter 26

Ariean calls the guides together
and notifies them that the
exercise will begin within a few
days. Supplies need to be pre-
positioned quickly and observers
need to be positioned to observe
the progress of the exercise
party. The guides gather the
supplies and take them to the
designated points for storage.
The guides who are to follow the
progress also take supplies for
themselves and their dogs.

Ariean thinks "the fox is afoot".
This is a term used in the past
for beginning the "hunt". In this
case the guides will be hunting as
LRPS (a term used in the past for
the long range patrols who
gathered information behind enemy
lines without making contact or
being detected). At some point,

the "hunt" will turn into what
used to be a "special forces"
mission, organizing and supporting
the underground forces behind
enemy lines. Now it will be
aiding those who are not known to
be friendly, in the wilderness.

Three weeks are to pass without
being detected or making contact.
Then several weeks will pass in
establishing contact on friendly
terms. How this is to be done
will be determined by the guides.
There is always a risk but the
guides are well trained to
minimize the risk.

   Ariean then goes to visit Andrew
and Mary to notify them. "The
exercise is beginning. It is
estimated that it will be four to
seven weeks before your guests
will arrive. In four weeks you
need to be close to home until

they arrive. A dog will be sent ahead a day or two before they are to arrive. The arrival will be scheduled for afternoon and the first meal will be an evening meal. The guests will need to retire early for a good night's sleep as they will have expended their energy getting here."

Andrew and Mary plan to have the rooms heated and the food ready when the guests arrived. They have organized the house to have a men's dormitory and a women's dormitory. They also have a small crib in the women's dormitory for the child. With sheets, blankets, bathing supplies and water to be heated, they are ready for their guests. The waiting begins.

Ariean leaves Andrew and Mary's home and goes to the second home, informing them, "Your guests will

be expected to arrive in five to
eight weeks. The guests will stay
with Andrew and Mary about a week
to recover from the exercise
before continuing on. A dog will
be sent to you when they arrive at
Andrew and Mary's home and the
guests will arrive about a week
later".

Chapter 27

Schort wakens Dan and Rani early.
They have the privilege of
preparing breakfast for Ayrd and
Lionia. Training always seems to
lead to doing something new and
interesting. This is to be their
test. They will be graded by Ayrd
and Lionia. It will be quite a
test as this is to be the way they
will meet Ayrd and Lionia.

Today is scheduled for a "shake
down". That is a phrase that they
have heard since they arrived
here. It originally meant that
the backpacks were checked or
"shook down" to reduce the weight
and remove all unnecessary items.
Today, the backpacks will be
carefully loaded and prepared for
the exercise. Ayrd will supervise
and decide if anything that had
been acquired is not needed. The

backpacks will be packed with items at the top that might need to be accessed quickly. Distributing the weight is also necessary. This makes a difference how fast the pack would wear out the carrier. For this exercise, a properly filled backpack will be absolutely necessary.

Ayrd awakened early. Yesterday had been a long day. His internal clock awakens him the same time each morning. It will be awhile before Lionia will awaken. Along with the long day before, the young boy had needed attention during the night. Ayrd's room is just down the hall and he was awakened by a crying baby during the night. He was able to go back to sleep as the baby quieted, but Lionia would have stayed awake and

cared for the baby until he went
to sleep.

It is close to noon when Lionia
makes her appearance. Mother and
baby are doing fine. The
breakfast meal has been timed and
is ready when they arrive for
breakfast. Ayrd hears them going
down the hall to the dining room
and joins them. After breakfast,
they clean the dishes and go to
the room where all the supplies
have been sorted and laid out.
Ayrd first adjusts the packs for
each individual. He then sets
about packing the packs,
distributing the weight in the
packs and also between the packs.
The men will carry heavier packs.
The women will carry less weight
but more bulk. Lionia will have
two packs, one for the gear and
another for the child. Ayrd and
Dan will also be equipped to carry

two packs. This will allow them
to carry the child also. By
sharing the time of carrying the
child Lionia will be able to
travel further each day. This is
important as there need to be
stops to feed and care for the
boy.

   After the packs are filled, the
travel clothing is inspected. It
is designed to provide warmth and
be able to release the heat when
traveling and their bodies were
burning the calories. The
clothing is designed to keep them
dry in both rain and snow. It is
durable and layered. Lionia also
has special clothing designed to
care for the boy. Rani and Lionia
retreat into another room and Rani
shows Lionia how to use the
clothing in order to take care of
the boy and still stay warm. The
society doesn't have this type of

clothing as mothers don't have the need to feed their babies after a couple of months.

The rest of the day is spent in relaxation and rest. The meals are prepared. Ayrd and Lionia are briefed on the food they will have on the exercise and how it will be prepared. They spend some time with Dan and Rani in the kitchen, cooking and cleaning.

Lionia is also able to get a nap in and get rested. That night they will all "hit the sack" early so they can get rested up. The following day, everything is double checked and the four are briefed on the exercise. Maps are gone over to indicate sources of water, dangerous cliffs and areas that were subject to flooding. Areas that are identified as good camping areas, sheltered from the wind, with water available, are also noted. Although they carry a small supply of water they will use the light water purification kit to safely use the water sources they encounter. This will reduce the weight they will be carrying.

Although Lionia taught geography and used maps, these maps are different. Ayrd is very familiar with the maps as he has used similar maps in his training. Dan and Rani have already had classes and have learned to read the maps. In their earlier exercises they have used maps as they practiced. It requires all of them, working together, to be successful in this exercise.

After the day of briefing Schort advises them to "hit the hay"

early again as they will be
leaving early the next morning.

Chapter 28

Five O'clock comes early. The
staff have already cooked
breakfast. The meal the previous
night was carb heavy. This
morning's breakfast is loaded with
protein. It will be a long day,
first of many. At five thirty
they are at the table eating. By
six thirty, the backpacks are on
their backs and the journey has
begun. They will be a fair
distance before the sun lightens
the sky. Anyone watching from the
Society would not notice them
leave. The air is brisk. The
days are shorter and the colors
are changing.
The days are still fairly warm,
but the nights are bordering cold.
They are well dressed for the
temperature. About an hour after
the sun rose into the sky they
stop to remove their outer coats.

The air is starting to warm up and they need to avoid working up a sweat.

Dan and Rani take the lead followed by Lionia. Ayrd takes the "trail" position. Dan and Rani have followed the set course for two days in their exercises to get ready. They can make better time with the knowledge of the trails the first two days. While traveling in strange lands, danger in front is more easily realized than danger in the rear. Ayrd keeps an eye on Lionia to make sure she is doing well. At the same time he regularly scans the terrain to the sides and rear. This technique allows him to see where they have been from another perspective, so the return trip will be easy. It also allows him to observe any animals and terrain features that have been missed in passing.

The first two weeks pass without incident. At the end of the second week, the nights are already getting bitter cold. They will be passing through an area that has been used for hunting years ago and has hunting "cabins". These are marked on the map for them. Although Ayrd does not intend to use the cabins as they will be confined indoors and not be able to hear or see anyone moving around them, he sees that Lionia and the child need the warmth of shelter.

The first cabin they come to has a fireplace and wood stacked outside. The wood is sheltered and dry. There is enough for two days. They need to continue on

their journey and a two day rest
will be plenty. As they enter the
cabin, they notice the fireplace
is set with wood and ready to be
lit. Whoever was there before
them left the cabin ready for the
next visitors. In the cellar they
find water for drinking. The
cellar is bermed and never gets
colder than 54 degrees Fahrenheit.

If there had been no firewood
they would have been comfortable
sleeping in the cellar. It is
warm compared to the outside night
air. They are able to wash
laundry and get the clothes dry
before continuing. This is
especially important for the
child.

The second night they repack
their supplies and refill their
water containers. They go to
sleep early to get a good rest.

After two nights and days of
rest and repair they start out
early on the morning of the third
day.

The map indicates the next cabin
to be a week away. Their camps
need to be well chosen to provide
enough warmth for them during the
night. They stop in an area that
has a supply of firewood. The
fires will not only be used for
cooking but for warmth at night.
They have warm sleeping bags and
ground pads. When the ground
allows they dig a pit long enough
and wide enough for each sleeping
bag. Coals from the fire are
placed in the pit and the coals
are be covered with several inches
of soil. Making sure they are
able to breathe fresh air this bed
provides more warmth. At other
times, when the weather demands
the use of a tent, they heat their

water and refill their containers.
The hot water containers provide
heat for the tent for several
hours in the night.

Chapter 29

It has been almost two months.
Supplies are running low. With
winter setting on early, they have
used more food to provide calories
than planned.

A cabin is only a day away on the
map. They start out early in
order to get to the cabin during
daylight. By late afternoon they
arrive at the cabin. There are
coals in the fireplace and the
cabin is warm. Wood had been
placed inside.

A quick survey of the perimeter
gives no indication that anyone is
still around. They enter the
cabin and add wood to the coals to
get a fire going. Off to the side
is a kitchen. There are aromas
coming from the kitchen. They
find a meal that is cooked and is
still hot. A note on the table

reads. "May the Lord bless you and keep you. May his produce feed you and strengthen you. May you rest with His peace."

Ayrd again goes outside and scouts the area. No one is to be found. Ayred thinks, "Whoever did this did not wait to be found. Why would anyone do this? How did anyone know we would be there at that time? Where did they go?"

Ayrd re-enters the cabin and joins the others for the meal. There is enough food for them to eat for two days. Trail food is also set aside for them to take with them on the next stage of their journey. The trail food is dried meat and fruit. Again, they find fresh water in a cellar and refill their water containers.

After two days, they start out early in the morning. The "early"

starts are getting later. They
plan to be hitting the trial as
the sky lightens. It is staying
darker longer. Shorter days mean
shorter trips each day. Windy
days slow them down. It is still
warmer during the day when the
sunny. Cloudy days are chilly.

Each morning they awake to find a
meal waiting for them. Ayrd finds
his thoughts going to the skills
of whoever is providing the food.
He finds no sign of when they come
or go. The first morning they
awaken to the smell of food there
is a note, "For your journey.
Don't take the pans. Eat and go.
Traveling light is good for the
soul". Each morning after that,
they "eat and go". Ayrd looked
back to each camp to see who would
come by and retrieve the pans. He
never saw anyone. Sometimes the
camp is visible for several hours.

Still he saw no one visit the camp.

Chapter 30

The weather is turning colder
faster. Winter is arriving sooner
this year than normal. It will
still be several days until they
will be able to use another cabin.
Toward the end of the day, they
spot a camp with tents set up and
a fire burning. Someone is moving
around the camp and seem to be
cooking. It is soon to be dark
and they can't risk going around
and finding another place to camp.

Ayrd approaches the camp
announcing himself. The others
wait at a distance. The man calls
out a welcome and Ayrd walks into
the camp looking for the party who
would be using the tents. The man
tells Ayrd that supper is almost
done and that he would be happy if
Ayrd and his party would join him.
Ayrd hears him say "join him", not

"them". Although this seems strange with the tents, Ayrd accepts and brings the others into the camp.

There they find a hot meal about ready to be served and tents already set up for them. The tents are a heavy material. They are much too heavy for back packing. Each tent has a liner and several inches of hay on the floor for insulation. There are two containers set to one side for the bricks. The containers won't get hot enough on the outside to start a fire, but will hold hot bricks. The bricks will then heat the tent through the night.

Backpackers wouldn't be able to carry the bricks so this was another benefit that they wouldn't have been able to do for themselves. The man has warmed

bricks and placed them in the
tents an hour before they arrive.
They are able to share a meal in
the "eating tent" before they turn
in. Both the "men's tent" and the
"women's tent" have their bricks
replaced with newly heated bricks
before turning in.

In the morning, breakfast is
waiting and the man is gone. A
note reads. "Thank you for being
my guests. I pray that you had
rest. Travel light as in flight
and trust the Lord for your
reward."

They were cold and tired when they
arrived. Ayrd did not get a name
or anything about their guest. He
had known that they would be
arriving there and had prepared
for them. That he is certain of.
How he knew and why he had

prepared are questions Ayrd intended to ask in the morning.

After breakfast, they clean the pots and pans, heating water over the fire, and start on their journey.

For several days, they "stumble upon" a camp like this one, with food and bricks ready. Each morning there is food ready to eat. After the first camp, they don't see the person who set up the camp. Their host is unknown.

When they arrive at the next cabin, they find it heated with food again ready. There are two hosts there this time. The man set about asking Ayrd and Dan why they are taking the journey, where they are headed, and what they are to accomplish. He posed the questions and then told Ayrd and Dan to study the questions and formulate their answers over night. They will discuss the next morning. The woman took Lionia and Rani to their room after the meal and posed the same questions to them.

Both the man and the woman tell them that they need to stay there for a few days in order to renew their energy and the time will be used to contemplate their next move. The man and the woman will see them each day and join in the discussion.

Chapter 31

The days pass quickly. The
discussions remind Ayrd and Lionia
of the Consults with P.T. The man
and the woman avoid suggestions
and input about themselves. They
guide the discussions so that the
travelers share their thoughts
with each other.

It is in this that Ayrd is able to
listen to Lionia and better
understand her need to raise the
child. Ayrd grows a strong desire
to be there to help her raise the
child.

It is in this that Dan and Rani
share their feeling of freedom to
grow and use their abilities.
This freedom is something they do
not want to give up to the
Society.

After several days of sharing Ayrd recalls the happy faces he had seen in over flights. He asks the man and woman if they know any of the Out Cast.

The man and the woman start with defining an Out Cast. "These are the ones that don't fit in the society. Some were able to stay out when the fences were built. Some were sent outside the fences by the Elite to die. Some found a way to get beyond the fences in order to find a new life."

The day was getting late and it is time to turn in. Discussion will continue tomorrow.

The next morning Ayrd is filled with questions. Dan and Rani have their questions also. When it comes time for Lionia to proclaim her questions she has only one, "What does God want for the boy?"

Somewhere in her contemplation the word "God" keeps coming from her youth.

Ayrd paused to consider. "God" had not been in his training. What does it mean? Who is she referring to? How is she going to get the answer? Did the two hosts know "God"? Could they find an answer? Dan and Rani have given thanks to "someone" for answering their petition for help. Could this person be "God"?

"Too many questions, … too few answers" is a saying from the past. They had never heard the saying until the hosts break in with "so many questions, so few answers. All things come in time."

"The Out Cast believe in God. They trust in God and follow his guidance in their dealings with each other and with others. When a person needs help, they work together to help that person. Each Out Cast acquires a variety of skills. Along with trades such as carpentry and metal working each Out Cast unit grows food for themselves and for sharing with those in need. They have freedom to move about and to change occupations. Skills are passed down to those interested in learning a trade. Teachers teach about the past trials and errors as well as the triumphs and tribulations of the old society. They learn about The Society and its functions. They reach out to provide for those in need both in the Out Cast and in The Society. Would you want to visit the Out Cast?"

Ayrd and Lionia look at each other and then at Dan and Rani. Dan and Rani look at each other

and then at Ayrd and Lionia.
Lionia was the first to speak. "I
believe that we are in agreement.
We would like to meet the Out
Cast." The others looked at
Lionia and nod their assent. The
boy just smiled.

The hosts say, "We will arrange
for you to meet the Out Cast.
Because of the weather you need to
plan to stay for an extended
period. They have prepared for
your visit and you will be
welcome. We will continue your
journey soon. Have you named the
boy? It is customary to introduce
everyone, including children, by
name."

Lionia says softly, "I have felt
his name should be Andrew."

Ayrd then said, "Then his name
shall be Andrew. His mother has
the right to name her child."

Chapter 32

The hosts prepare a final meal
this morning. Supplies are packed
and everyone is ready to continue
on the journey. At the table this
morning is a man introduced as
Ariean. They are told he will
accompany them to their next stop
with his companion, Alehandra.
"Alehandra will help carry the
load so we can move faster. She
can be obstinate and stubborn but
she is also invaluable for
journeys like this. I advise you
to always stay in front of her and
treat her nice and she will help
take care of you." Ariean advised.

They all looked around the room
wondering why Alehandra had not
joined them. After the meal, they
quickly dress and carry their
packs out to the outbuilding where
Alehandra is waiting. Ariean

quickly attaches two packs and places Lionia in a saddle with Andrew. There is a dog nearby. Ariean says, "I will lead Alehandra. Ayrd, take the lead and follow the dog". They start out with the dog leading, then Ayrd, Dan, Rani, Ariean, with Alehandra, carrying Lionia and Andrew, taking up the rear guard. The pace is faster. At midday they come to a camp site with food prepared as before. This allows rest and warmth. Then they continue on their journey.

Evening is approaching and darkness is starting to blanket the land when they see a building fairly close. This must be their stop for the night. Smoke is coming out of a chimney and there is a glimmer of light in a window. The building seems to say "I am waiting for you to warm you and comfort you. You are welcome here."

The dog runs ahead as if he knows this is where they are to stay and to announce their arrival. When they approach the house Ariean stops in the yard and rings a bell that hangs on a gate a ways from the house. The door opens and the occupants come out.

Andrew calls out, "The barn is ready, come with us and unload your gear". Andrew and Mary lead them to the barn and help unload. Ariean introduces Ayrd and Dan, Rani, Lionia and Andy. Mary helped Lionia and Andy down and take them and Rani to the house.

The men carry the gear to an attached house. They unpack and get everything situated, adding wood to the fire, then they also go to the main house as the meal is ready.

After the meal, Andrew says, "You are welcome. The attached house is yours to stay while you are here. We plan on having meals here and anticipate that you have questions that we will try to answer. You have had a long journey. Rest tonight and we will come together tomorrow and talk."

After they left Mary looks at Andrew and said "Lionia and Andy?" Andrew responds, "We have placed our trust in God. Have we not asked for assurance that our daughter is O.K.? This could be our answer. Let us be patient in understanding. As yet, we do not know the relationship between these four adults, only that Lionia is Andy's mother and that all have arrived here safely before the hard winter sets in. We are blessed with the opportunity to host them and to get to know them. That is enough for tonight. Tomorrow brings a new day and new information."

Mary lay awake until early morning before finding sleep. So many desires to know and so much anxiety that, indeed, this is her Lionia keeps her awake. Andrew gets little sleep also. He has the same concern, that their prayers are being answered. About the time Mary found sleep Andrew gets up and starts preparing for the day. He goes to the barn and feeds the stock and Alehandra. Alehandra gets special treatment as she worked hard the day before and will have a long journey today. As Andrew is finishing chores Ariean joins him. Andrew greets him with, "You are a

blessing to all with your caring
and work. You need to get started
quickly. Come into the house and
share some food with me before you
leave." Andrew and Ariean go to
the house and eat the food Andrew
had prepared. Then Ariean saddles
Alehandra and starts home with
dog.

Chapter 33

A new day starts with the sun
starting to color the sky with a
blue glow. Andrew has food
prepared and the table set when
Mary makes her appearance. Andrew
remarks, "Sleep well my dear?"

Mary answers "The sleep I got was
good. Thank you for letting me
sleep as you did the chores and
fixed the meal. Has Ariean left
for home?"

"Yes. It is a long journey. By
starting early he should be there
by tonight."

Mary says, "I wonder when our
guests will awake."

Andrew responds, "I believe that
Ayrd has been up for a while.
Someone stoked the fire and he
seems to be the one who gets up
early from the reports we have

had. The house should be getting warm and coming alive about now."

Andrew had correctly anticipated the activity in the guest house. At that very moment, all are up and have finished dressing. Andy is hungry and is being fed. It will only be a few minutes and they will arrive for breakfast.

The "journey" from the guest house to the main house is through a connecting room. They do not need to put heavy clothing on for this trip. Dan escorts Rani. Ayrd arrives, carrying Andy, with Lionia. Andrew and Mary quietly notice the tenderness with which Ayrd carries Andy and the quiet formality with which Dan cares for Rani.

Andrew greets them with, "Thank you for joining us. We pray that you had a restful and comfortable

243

night's sleep. Did Andy behave himself so you could get a good rest, Lionia?"

Lionia sees his smile at this comment and smiles back responding, "Andy behaved himself very well and we both got a fair amount of rest. Thank you for the baby supplies you provided."

"You are entirely welcome, now let us eat," responds Mary. Over the meal Andrew asks, "Dan how did you happen to make the journey?" Dan explains, "Both Rani and I were put on leave as our machinery was not working. The weeks with reduced rations weakened us. Then one day one of the Elite offered us a job on the border. That led to this exercise and our being here".

After the meal, Andrew asks Ayrd, "What training do you have that put you on path to getting here?" Ayrd explains, "I was chosen to be of the Guard Cast and was trained as a special class pilot. I was sent to the Farm to serve as a donor for a replacement child. The consult named P.T. sent me on the exercise to watch over and help a woman and child. Later, Dan and Rani were added to the exercise".

Andrew waits for Lionia. Mary is getting anxious. Andrew turns to Lionia and asks about her training and path to get here. Lionia goes into detail about her early childhood and the parents she knew briefly. While listening to the others, she observed Andrew and Mary. Listening to them brought a familiar tone to her ears. There is … something about them. Now, explaining her childhood, she sees a light in Mary's eyes grow bright. There is an understanding glowing through.

 Lionia continues to explain her education and her Cast role as a teacher. She continued to take care of herself physically and mentally. In a way that she doesn't fully understand, she had maintained her spirituality. Lionia explains, "I was chosen to produce a child for the society. I developed a deep love for the child and wished the child could have parents as I had when I was little. Something in my memory encouraged me to name the boy Andrew. It is a name that has fond memories". She continued to explain, "I had accidentally met Ayrd waiting for my consult. That we were both chosen for the exercise is a mixture of fortune

and enigma. It is fortune as I
had wanted to know more about him.
It is an enigma as I am at a loss
why we were chosen for the
exercise. It makes sense that
Ayrd would be chosen but a mother
with a young child doesn't make
sense".

Chapter 34

Andrew thanks them for filling
in the background and begins to
share his and Mary's path.

"We were young and Mary was a
Teacher Cast. I was of the
Building Cast. We grew to care
for one another as I noticed Mary
carrying both books and her food
allotment home and offered to help
her. We secretly married and had
a child. We were able to use
vacation time and work schedules
to have the child and keep her
hidden for two years. When we
were discovered, the child was
taken for training. This was the
last we had seen her. We were cut
off rations and lost our jobs. A
Fli helped us to the border and
the Elect brought them to this
area, helped them get established
in a home and taught them the

skills necessary to both survive and be able to contribute to others in need".

Andrew then explains, "The vast majority of the Out Cast are the Elect. There are Elect in the society who are underground and are cut off when discovered. Some of them are in the Elite Cast and have been assigned as Flis".

Andrew pauses and looks at Mary before continuing. He then spoke in a soft voice, almost a whisper, "Our daughter was named Lionia".

While he said this both he and Mary looked directly at Lionia. Andrew drew a breath and continued, "We have asked God daily to send us information about our daughter. It seems that our prayers have been answered."

At this point Mary and Lionia go to each other and embrace. After what seems like an eternity they sit down beside each other and Andrew continues. "One of the elect in the society discerned your need to raise your son. It was decided that the son should be raised by his mother and father. The exercise was set up to see if the father would bond with his child and the mother. The need to get Dan and Rani to safety coincided with the planned exercise. It was decided that Ayrd had the best skills to make the journey as smooth as possible. Therefore, he was positioned as the guide. Ayrd, as both father and guide was the key to the exercise being successful."

Lionia looks at Ayrd during this talk and finds the reason she felt the need to get to know him. Her prayers were answered by the God she had trusted. Ayrd looks at Andy and thinks, "This is my son! The attraction I have to get to know Lionia is because she carried my son!" Ayrd thinks of the times he watched her from afar and found her to be poetry in his life. That "something" that he worked to define in her is her love for the child and her love for everyone. She is filled with caring and love. That grew as they made their journey. Although, making the journey without the help of Rani would have been much more difficult". Rani was able to help with Andy when Ayrd was busy.

Chapter 35

The following days Andrew and Mary share with their guests just how the Elect society functioned. There is sharing and help. Everyone works at something and everyone raises some produce. Everyone is encouraged to spend some time with God each day.

Andrew tells Dan and Rani that a home was prepared for their initial stay at another location and that they will be moving there fairly soon. The house that they are currently occupying was built for Ayrd, Lionia and Andy until they can get situated.

The Elect set aside food and supplies to last them through the winter. During this time they will learn more skills to start out.

Andrew explains to Dan and Ayrd the function of each building, "The barn is a shelter for the livestock. At one end of the barn is a house for the fowl. This has a door so they can get out during the day. We raise a combination of chickens, ducks, and geese.

The operation is three levels. The eggs are used for food unless they are fertilized. Then the eggs are incubated to raise another generation of fowl. The birds are used to provide meat and the geese provide down for insulation in their clothing and the bed tick. The barn also houses some cattle. Milk cows are kept and milked daily. Excess milk, in the winter, is frozen and transported to those who have a need.

The Elite live by building basic
structures for storage and
survival. The ice cellar
construction is covered in depth.
First is digging a hole in the
ground (side of a hill if
possible). Then the rooms are
laid out and straw bales are made
for the walls. Timbers are used
both inside and outside of the
bales to protect them from
moisture. Dirt is then graded on
the outside to insulate the bales
with four feet of dirt. Inside
the bales a runway is constructed
to contain ice. This runway has a
drain to take the melted ice to a
cistern. Inside the runway is a
storage room. The ice keeps the
room near freezing. Each winter,
water is taken from a nearby
stream and allowed to freeze in
blocks. The blocks are stored in
the runways until full. The ice

keeps the cellar cold through the hottest summers. This is our natural freezer.

The house is built so that fresh air comes from the outside through a tunnel and enters the house by the fire place. In the winter the fire place heats the 54-degree air to a comfortable warmth.

Off to the side is the garden and orchard. We work hard during the summer. The good part is that all the work is within a few yards of home. Others raise cattle and hunt wild game for the Elect.

In the corner of the barn I have a workshop. I manufacture furniture for those in need. The workshop is heated and I spend many days during the winter working there. The day starts with chores to feed and water the animals and fowl. Then we eat breakfast. After breakfast, I work in the shop while Mary constructs clothing, blankets (filled with down), and other cloth items that are needed.

Chapter 36

   Back in society, at the
Communications Cast, Andi reads
the morning reports. (The gardens
of the elderly are not producing.
The elderly are starving. Workers
are attacked in the streets on
their way home from the food
distribution centers by those who
do not qualify for food
distribution. The injured soon
become unemployed and do not
qualify for food distribution.
Areas of society are not
functioning). Andi can not report
these situations. Her job is to
continue to support the Elite with
news that projects a successful
society.

   This is a demanding job, not so
much for the physical or mental
exercises as for the stress of any
possible error that will lead to

be sent to the Out Cast. An Out
Cast can not go to the food
distribution point or live in Cast
housing, or use transporters or be
productive in any Cast. They are
simply shunned from society.

The only survival for an Out
Cast is to make contact with the
Elect. The Elect are those who
refuse to give up the old ways and
keep a belief in God. They choose
to be Out cast rather than submit
to the Chosen One and the Elite.
The Elect secretly grow their own
food, make their own clothing and
make primitive shelters where they
live on the fringes of society.
All Out Casts are welcomed and
taught skills that help them
survive outside the society.

Andi looks at the message from
The Chosen One. Her neighborhood
is noted for crime. She doesn't

know her neighbors as the housing has been arranged so each person lives among those in other Casts, and other shifts. As such, few are home when she is home. Some who are home are on different shifts and are sleeping.

The youth run the streets when the adults are working. At age fifteen, they have four days of school and three days of work a week. This lasts until age twenty-two. Each day is ten hours. In the old days, school was five days a week and classes were only seven hours a day. Now there is more classroom time each week and full employment of the fifteen to twenty-two year old individuals. When their required education ends at twenty-two they can continue to take classes in their off-time. They continue to work in the job they are trained

in unless they can convince the
Elite that they are qualified for
a Cast that needs more members.

Chapter 37

It is time for Dan and Rani to
move to their location. Ariean
and Alehandra arrive at dusk. They
will stay the night and prepare to
leave the next morning.

The sky is beginning to light
when Andrew and Ariean saddle the
horses and Alehandra. Supplies
are taken for a day's ride. Dan
and Rani load their packs and are
ready to depart. All share
breakfast before their departure.
Ayrd and Lionia say, "Plan to see
us when spring comes" and "travel
with God in your pocket".

Ariean and Alehandra lead the
way and Dan and Rani ride off with
the daybreak. The days are
getting shorter as winter
approaches. They make good time.
Stopping for lunch they find
another meal already prepared for

them. Hot food on a cold trip is
welcome. The fire also gives some
heat. Ariean remind them not to
get too hot as to sweat. The
evaporation from the sweat as they
continue on the trip will make
them cold and can cause health
problems. "Warm your feet and
hands, but don't get too hot
here," Ariean warns.

When they had been walking they
produced heat with the exercise.
Riding makes a difference. They
are less active and it is harder
to stay warm. The saddles are
covered with wool and the chaps
they ware on their legs have a
wool liner. Their coats are down
filled and their hats and gloves
are wool. They still feel the
cold, although they are fairly
comfortable. The warm fire does
feel good, but they follow
Ariean's directions and don't get

too close. The rest of the trip
goes without incident. They stop
occasionally to watch deer,
coyotes, quail, and pheasants.
Ariean uses the opportunity to
explain what they use each of the
wild creatures for. Then they
continue the journey.

Night will be falling shortly.
The western sky is ablaze with
red, yellow, orange and silver.
Soon the sun will set. They are
arriving at their destination.
They see two houses here. These
are not connected as those at
Andrew and Mary's are. Ariean
leads them to the yard of the
oldest house and rings the bell in
the yard.

They are to stay here until their
skills allow them to settle on
their own.

Chapter 38

Andrew and Mary thank God for
sending Ayrd and Lionia to them.
Why they were chosen to host them
does not matter.

Andrew starts with, "Why we have
chosen this path and the history
leading up to "The Society" is
important for you to understand.
Mary has researched and has
volumes of information. I am
going to let her cover this
material for you."

Mary starts with, "There are
several areas of focus. There are
the political, societal, economic,
religious, legal, and moral
aspects that make up a society.
Each of these is important as to
its impact on and relevance with
the others. Ideally, everyone in
a society is moral. Everybody
helps everybody else and no one

hurts anyone else. Each
individual has risen to the state
of agape. While some rise to this
level many are stuck somewhere
below or are on a journey to agape
and have not arrived.

Because the human condition is
varied and wants and needs are
varied those who live together in
a society need rules that define
proper and improper behavior.
This is where religious teachings
come into play. These are the
undercurrent of moral teachings
that have survived thousands of
years and predate laws.

People have a choice of whether
to subscribe to religious precepts
and teachings. Some would deny
all such teachings. Because some
seek to change the society by
violating moral attribute laws
that have been instituted by

societies to regulate behavior and to provide a certain safety and security to the members of that society.

These laws are promulgated by those citizens of the society who respond to a perceived need. The purpose of the laws is to keep order and protect those who would be victims.

The economic elements depend on work ethics, abilities and a bit of luck. These attributes allow some to grow a business more than others and to have more assets than others. Those who have the willingness, ability and opportunity provide employment for others who can do the work involved in making the business a success.

The political element grows as a society grows. When there are more citizens than can meet together and handle the laws and ethics of society representatives are chosen to make decisions for the people and keep the society running to secure the rights of all members.

As time goes on the Legal element starts giving special rights to special elements of society. There are elements who need special protection and there are those who don't, but demanded it. Some of these elements successfully gain an advantage by getting special protection and denying others their rights. The Black Robes rule that this is proper and the representatives rule that this is needed.

Times change. Marriage becomes a mere formality to be used or not.

Children are raised without both parents. This causes them to grow without the ethics that two parents provide. Marriage is defined as a social contract rather than a family unit.

 Children are disposable. Life is considered valuable only when the Representatives and Black Robes said it is. As groups of individuals are marginalized, starting with babies in the womb, more and more are allowed to be terminated.

 The laws stop protecting. The lawmakers start choosing who are to be protected. The citizens slowly lose their protections. The right to free speech is the first to be attacked. Next, religious expression is limited to inside churches, synagogues and

religious meeting places. Then
religious expression is forbidden.

 When the citizens protest,
martial law is established and
elections are halted. Those in
power assume the role of being the
Elite Cast on a stage of society
politic. They decide that protest
indicates the members of society
do not have the ability to
continue to participate in
decision making, and start making
the decisions for them.

 After reducing the value of
life, the Elite promise to take
care of everyone. In order to do
this, they attack those who build
businesses and provide jobs. In
the early days, they established
regulations that make it difficult
to stay in business, then attacked
the businesses for not being able
to succeed. After that they

started taking over businesses
claiming they were "too big to
fail". This was accepted by the
citizens as needed. The dam
holding the Elite back cracked and
before they knew it the citizens'
lives were totally controlled by
the Elite."

Chapter 39

Ayrd asks, "What was the rule of law back then?"

Mary answered "They called it the Constitution of the United States. It was devised to hold thirteen independent states together under a limited Federal government. The Federal government would protect the states from internal or external attacks, providing the security needed to prosper. It would also regulate the commerce between the states so that commerce could move freely and give each state the ability to buy and sell between each other without tariffs and restrictive regulations.

Each state was given the power to operate independently with all the powers (like a separate nation) not expressly reserved to the

Federal Government. Each state had the right to make its own laws and provide for its own defense. Over time the states gave up more and more of their power to the Federal Government. The people wanted to be taken care of and allowed the government to harm the businesses that provided employment until the government needed to "step in to save their jobs".

By the time the people realized that the government solution was worse for them, it was too late. The Constitution had been "re-defined" by the Elite and Black Robes until the meaning had been entirely changed and no guarantees remained."

Mary continued the lesson. "It all started with the idea that the guarantees of the Constitution

could be used for special groups
even when they ended the rights of
other groups. First, the Black
Robes ruled that blacks could
legally be slaves. Their rights
were only those the owners gave
them. Then the Black Robes ruled
that employers had no rights.
They were required to pay a
guaranteed salary independent of
the productivity of the employee.
They could only hire those the
government would allow them to. If
the employee were fired, the
employer had to pay unemployment
benefits for a period of time.

Then the Black Robes ruled that
children were not protected under
the Constitution until they were
viable. They overlooked the law
that defined viability as the
ability to change, move and grow,
which starts when the egg is
fertilized. They overlooked that

the baby has separate genes and traits from the mother immediately and ruled that the baby wasn't a person until sometime later.

The "sometime later" was not defined by the Black Robes and there were powerful Elite who stopped the Elect from defining a person with Constitutional protections. Meanwhile mothers continued to be maimed, harmed and abused by abortions while the some died with their children as a result of the abortion." As the mothers suffered the results of abortions and children died, the Elite continued to sell the procedure as "safe and legal". While the procedures were neither safe nor legal the elite continued to deceive the society.

In order to reduce the "unwanted" pregnancies the Elite

made it illegal to naturally bear
children. The farm was instituted
to control the birth rate and
provide for the continuance of
society.

Chapter 40

Christian religions were a
problem. They taught that the
government should protect all
persons as the Constitution
stated. In order to form "The
Society," it was imperative that
Christians be marginalized, then
limited, then outlawed. Freedom
from religion became the pass
word."

Mary continued, "Christian
religions started the first
schools and hospitals. They were
first in adoption services and
feeding the poor and hungry.
Slowly, the Chosen One and the
Elite Cast took over schools, then
social services, then hospitals.
The Christians were attacked for
not being open to changes. They
worked against the Elite abortion
plan. They worked against the

Elite project to marginalize marriage and families. They worked to keep their schools and hospitals. This was a thorn in the side of the Elite.

The Elite uses their schools to teach the young not to accept the values of their parents and grandparents. The Constitution was taken out of the education system. As voters became less aware of the rights in the Constitution they voted for what the Elite told them was good for them. This led to more control by the Elite and fewer rights for the individuals."

Ayrd commented, "We are taught only what we need to serve the Elite in the Cast we are assigned to. Without a broad basis to go from we are helpless to change."

Andrew then added, "We have books you can study. Getting to

know the old system and the
strengths it had will take time.
For now we have started to open
the door to your learning.
Another point we will cover is the
current status of both The Society
and the Elect."

Chapter 41

Ayrd commented, "With
Christians being a threat to The
Society I don't understand why our
fly-overs are only to observe and
never harm."

Andrew explained, "The fence
keeps the Christians from
infecting The Society. As long as
there is no large scale movement
close to the fence, there is no
threat to The Society. The Out
Cast grow more food, and produce,
and meat than The Society grows.
The Elite and the Chosen One
receive the best produce from the
Out Cast for their use. In
return, the Out Cast are able to
import dry goods and metals to
make and repair machinery. As
long as the lower Casts don't know
that the Elite are better fed,
there is no problem. The Guard

Cast reports not only when the Out Cast gather together and how many but the photos record the successful farming. The Elite Cast quietly protect their source of food."

"There are also skills that had been lost in society that the Out Cast preserves. These skills allows the Elite to live better lives. They have finer clothes, finer furniture, unique furnishings like plates and tableware that are used for home cooked meals like you are experiencing here. They also find joy in literature that can not be found in The Society. The Out Cast provide them with a level of Comfort that The Society can not."

"The over flights serve a dual purpose. The pictures give them the information on the progress and success of crops. At the same time their distrust of the Out Cast requires them to insure there is no large assembly close to the fence. If the Out Cast gets close to the fence they fear that they will be attacked or those in The Society will find out about our existence. This will lead to dissatisfaction when those in The Society realize those on the outside are happy."

The sky is growing dim. After supper they retire for the night. Ayrd takes a copy of the Constitution to his room and spends time studying it. There are many questions that arise in his mind. Where is the fabric that held it together and why was the fabric torn?

Chapter 42

Ayrd notices that each
representative (both the House and
Senate) and the President took an
oath to support and defend the
Constitution. Why hadn't they
done so? He noticed that the
Courts had the responsibility to
keep them from wandering from
their Constitutional
responsibilities. Why hadn't they
done so?

It took over one hundred years
to diminish the Constitution.
Ayrd reads the history thinking of
the example of a forest. "Each
day a nail is be driven into a
tree. Over time trees are to be
removed because they die. The
nail is not noticed. The dead
tree is noticed. Everyone agrees
that the dead trees need to be
removed. Those who drove the

nails point out the need and are allowed to remove the trees. One day the forest is gone and those who approved the removal of the trees are blamed".

Over time those elected to protect citizens' rights and support and defend the Constitution redefined the rights until the rights are abolished. It started with the rights and responsibilities of the various government bodies. Rights were granted that were not given by the Constitution and there was always a "good reason". Then rights given to the people were slowly taken away "for their safety". Eventually, the right to work became the responsibility to work. The right to strive for success and individual initiative was denied as "greedy". The right to build a business was denied as "corrupt". The right to bear arms, to regulate the power of the militia, was denied as the right to bear arms was to be determined to belong only to the Elite and their militia.

Ayrd finds in his studies of the historical downfall of what had been known as the greatest nation, a systematic setting of one group against another. The elementary "divided we fall, united we stand" had been proved. The people had been systematically divided. Instead of working to unite and strengthen the nation as it had been in the first hundred and forty years, the government worked to destroy the wealth of the nation, the initiative and productivity of its people.

One of the first to go was the belief that depending on the state was anathema. Self reliance was the goal of every citizen. This was assailed as not being charitable (a basic dogma of many religions). Just as a religion was to take care of the poor and elderly, the government assumed the right to do this. It was accepted as religious leaders didn't believe they could provide the help that was needed. What they approved of as a temporary measure became imbedded in the government. It became a part of life to be taken care of by the government. In many cases this became a generational life. As families felt the right to be taken care of, the need to be self reliant was diminished and often discouraged. The government had employees who would go so far as to encourage workers to quit their employment and get better benefits

from the government for not
producing.

Chapter 43

The next morning Andrew and Mary continue their lessons.

Ayrd comments, "I have studied parts of the Constitution last night and have read a historical account of the downfall. Why would people allow this to happen to them?"

Mary mentions, "Sickness begins with an oversight, or simply not understanding what is happening. Sometimes we do not follow sanitary procedures and it causes us to get sick. Sometimes we are simply in the wrong place when the virus is there and we get sick.

These things creep up on us and sometimes they can kill us. This is what happened to our society. The Elect managed to stay away from the pull to be taken care of.

They were able to establish a Christian society outside of The Society. By retaining the need to be self-sufficient and willing to help each other in work, prayer, sacrifices, and play we have the strength of love and compassion. We have the knowledge of accomplishment and worthiness."

Lionia quietly listened. She is also somewhat distracted by Andy's activity. She says, "I have experienced both. As a child, I felt the security and comfort of parents. When the Elite Cast took me away from them, I experienced the mechanization of The Society. How it got to that point I never knew. I do know that I have lived years yearning for the family love that I had known. I have felt that a part of my life was missing. When I gave birth to Andy, I knew that he needed a father and mother to grow as a strong and healthy child. I asked the universal listener to allow me to raise him.

That prayer was heard as we were led out into the wilderness on a journey to freedom. This journey let us experience that hardships are made easier with help from friends. In our case the friends were, initially, those we had never even seen. They sheltered us and provided food and heat to make our journey successful. This was the opposite of how our companions, Dan and Rani were treated by The Elite. In The Society, those not producing are easily forgotten."

Andrew continued, "The way of the Elect is the way the country grew to be the best society ever produced. Everyone was guaranteed

the right to work; to be self
sufficient while helping each
other when crops were bad or
machinery broke down. When
sickness or injury came, visiting
the neighbors meant visiting with
medicines, helping with chores,
and tending the crops and animals.
There is great satisfaction in
being able to help others just
because you want to. Being forced
to do anything robs us of the
grace and fulfillment of doing
something special. Here it is a
personal decision. We help each
other because we want to."

Chapter 44

Ayrd asks, "Why did the
Constitution have amendments?"
Mary responds, "Those who wrote
the Constitution knew the basics
for governing needed to be spelled
out. The Senate gave equal
representation to the states. The
House gave representation, based
on population, to the people. The
President would represent all the
people and act as a check on the
houses of Congress with a veto
power. If the Congress and
President failed to stay with the
law, a court was established to
rule whether the legislation was
constitutionally valid.

They knew that the basics
weren't enough and that time would
reveal needs to protect the people
so they included the requirements
for passing amendments and

enhancing the Constitution to
better protect the people.

As time went on judges were
appointed to the court who varied
in their rulings. They changed
laws to be what they wanted
instead of ruling to protect the
Constitution. This led to both an
ignorance of the Constitution and
the loss of its protections."

Lionia asks how this had
happened. Mary answers, "They
stopped teaching the Constitution
in schools so the people didn't
know what they had or what they
were missing. They forbade prayers
in schools and some schools even
forbad reciting the Pledge of
Allegiance, which was a document
people recited where they made a
pledge, or promise, to be faithful
to the flag of United States of
America and to the society and

principals for which that flag
stood. These worked together to
lead the populace down a road that
said, "we are in charge, follow
what we say!" and the majority
didn't know any better.

However," she continued, "There
were some parents who taught their
children at home, in parochial
schools or in private schools and
successfully fought the
requirements to send their
children to the government
schools. These learned the
Constitution and wanted their
rights restored. Most of these
ended up with the Elect."

Ayrd responds, "The Constitution
specifically denied the ability of
the Government to infringe on the
free exercise of religion or to
establish a religion".

Mary continues, "The attack on religious beliefs started as marginalization. The courts demanded that religions not be visible or active in society. By not being recognized by the government as a religion, the government was able to establish its own religion and call it "freedom from religion". This was started as "separation of church and state". The churches were denied their right to be active in the society and the government grew its religion without opposition. It really was a religion because it was a belief about the existence of God and the relationship with mankind. The belief was that there is no God (in opposition to all major belief systems) and that mankind has no relationship with a God or even a

valid existence beyond an
undefined essence.

They went further. They
instituted elements of
Christianity. They took care of
the poor, provided housing,
clothing, health care, helped the
elderly, and provided jobs and
education. These were all
elements of religions and were
accepted by the society."

Lionia remarked, "But what about
families? Why didn't they
survive?"

Mary responded, "First, they
convinced women that they had the
right to sex outside of marriage
just as men did. It is interesting
to note that neither sex had the
right, but the courts would rule
for the man in many cases saying
that the woman "asked for it".
This was true in cases of rape as

well as what they called "date
rape". If they were under the age
of majority, meaning the law
considered them not to be legal
adults, it was "statutory rape,"
but the courts did not uphold the
law. Women were getting pregnant
when they weren't legally able to.
The government decided that they
couldn't stop the pregnancies, so
they promoted the aborting of the
child's life and called it for
"the health of the mother". In
many cases, the operation caused
the woman to be sterilized. There
were symptoms of despair, suicide,
hearing a baby cry and finding no
baby there, and a feeling of
having lost a child. These were
not acknowledged as the child was
aborted "for the health of the
mother".

When promoting "safe sex" caused
more pregnancies chemicals were

introduced to "prevent
pregnancies". They caused a
conceived child to be unable to
thrive and be aborted early. They
also increased the rate of cancer
among women. Again, the standard
phrase of the Elite was "for the
health of the mother". It was
documented that a third of women
using the chemicals got breast
cancer, which was far above those
who didn't use the chemicals.
This thirty percent was determined
by the Elite to be an acceptable
risk for "the health of the
mother".

Mary continues, "The next step
was banning all pregnancies except
for those offered by the state.
The reason was "to address the
overpopulation problem". At the
time, this came about all of the
western countries were
experiencing a negative

replacement rate. As they decided who would be offered the opportunity, the choices excluded many minority classes. The real goal was to cleanse the society. This actually started earlier with abortions being promoted primarily among the poor and minority communities and poor and minority nations."

"The impact on families was predetermined. There was no need for families when the Elite would take care of the children and determined who would bear children."

Chapter 45

Ayrd asks, "Didn't the fourteenth amendment state 'nor shall any State deprive any person of life, liberty or property'?

My study of the elements of Biology taught me that the life of an animal begins at the fertilization of the egg. In humans, this is called conception. I had another course in Genetics where we learned that a child at conception is a unique individual with attributes different from both parents. Why didn't the courts protect the child?"

Mary responds , "The first step to doing away with a class of persons is to marginalize them. That means you teach that they aren't fully human. If they had said the baby wasn't human, there would have been uproar. By saying that the baby was "only a fetus, a blob of tissue," the reality of a living baby was obscured for many. The judges ruled that the baby was not protected by the Constitution because she wasn't "fully human". Prior to that, the ability to change, grow and move defined the viability of a child. These begin at conception."

Lionia asks "Where did this idea come from? I have felt the presence of a baby with me from the moment of conception".

Andrew indicates that this question requires an explanation based on Philosophy. "There are those who deny the existence of God. Some of them conceptualize that there are several things that are necessary to be fully human. There has to be an existence of a human body. In addition to that there has to be a logical ability and the ability to function independently, being the essence of an individual. Those who define the baby to not be fully human have subscribed to this belief system. The government adopted it and made it law. Although it was never determined at what point in growth the essence is present the law was upheld. Age has no bearing. If an individual is not capable of living independently the essence has not been achieved or has been lost. At this point the person's life can be legally ended. The person can be aborted. The government requires persons to sign "end of life" agreements that allow the government to terminate those who are not able to take care of themselves."

Andrew continued, "Then there were the leaders who were elected by those who voted without knowing the dangers they were getting into. They elected leaders who violated the Constitution, believed they were elected to run the country instead of serve the people under the Constitution."

Ayrd asks, "Didn't those who ignored and substituted different laws for the Constitution in fact violate the fourteenth amendment against having participated in a "rebellion or other crime" when their oath of office was to preserve, protect, and defend the Constitution of the United States, and they failed to do so? Why weren't they impeached and removed for high crimes and misdemeanors?"

Andrew responds, "Those responsible for upholding the oath and impeaching were also guilty and would not proceed."

Mary adds, "The Constitution was formed from hundreds of years experience in Europe. The first schools on Democracy and being a Republic were formulated there. The dangers of a state religion were experienced there through persecutions. The dangers of an unarmed populace were experienced where governments were taken over and militaries used to rule the people. The dangers of a strong central government were known and the Constitution addressed all of these. Over time the citizens weren't taught the meaning behind these rights. They came to believe these rights were no longer needed and freely gave them

up to a strong central government
until no rights were left."

Chapter 46

Postscript:

As this story is told, somewhere in the future, by a Fli, we remember that Eleven score and six years ago our forefathers founded this great nation. We have exceeded the length any Democracy had existed. This gives credence to having a Republic, which is more stable than a Democracy. Now we are engaged in a great trial testing whether this nation or any nation so governed can long endure. The preservation of the truths and principals endowed by our creator is subject to the will and understanding of the people.

The ability to live the religious beliefs handed down is under attack. The ability to defend ourselves against the government is being attacked. The

right to the freedom of speech
aimed at unruly and dishonest
government policies is being
attacked. There are those who
would jail anyone speaking against
the government. The freedom to
remove those from office who
violate their oath has been lost.
The recourse to the courts is
subject to political whim.

   When was the last time you read
the Constitution, and studied the
reason for each article, each
amendment? When was the last time
you took time to understand the
position of the candidates, check
their record, check the platform
of their party, and vote? When
was the last time you helped your
neighbor who was in need? When
was the last time you stood up for
States rights and limited Federal
Government? With every right is a
responsibility. Every Citizen

over the age of 18 has the right to vote. Each has the responsibility to study the candidates and vote. Each voter always wins. Having voted, the voter has fulfilled an obligation of citizenship and this is a winning hand. Sometimes the winning candidate doesn't live up to our hopes but we win when we fulfill our responsibilities. When a candidate we didn't vote for wins we still win. We have done our obligation.

This is a test! How will you complete it? Are you registered? Will you study the issues and assess the candidates? Will you vote? Have you paid your dues to be a citizen? Have you met you obligation?

As a society we depend on each other. When I don't do my

obligation I harm everyone else.
All it takes for bad government to
prosper is for good citizens to do
nothing. Without full
participation the few rule and
impose their will on the majority.
The "99%" is actually 51% of the
45% who actually vote. That's
22.55% of the citizens eligible to
vote who determine the direction
of this society. If you are not
in that 22.55% you are hurting the
rest of society. It is not those
who vote who are the problem. It
is those who do not vote that
allow the problem. We depend on
each eligible citizen to keep a
strong and free society. Do you
do your part?

Author:

The author, writing under the pseudo name "Tunes A Chord" has chosen the name to signify working together (Tunes) in A society (Chord).

He volunteered as a Red Cross Water Safety Instructor and Water Safety Instructor Trainer for 27 years.

He served in the Military, active and Reserve, for 27 years. The oath taken is the same oath taken by Congress and the President, to "support and defend the Constitution of the United States against all enemies, foreign and domestic".

While in the Military the Author studied Law, receiving a Law Diploma, and served as a Senior Legal Clerk in a JAG Detachment.

Thomas Deaver is currently a small business owner.

Made in the USA
Monee, IL
17 September 2022

13603312R00184